THE ICE PALACE

Tarjei Vesaas

THE ICE PALACE

Translated by Elizabeth Rokkan

PETER OWEN · LONDON

PETER OWEN PUBLISHERS
73 Kenway Road London SW5 0RE

Translated from the Norwegian *Is-slottet*
English translation first published 1966
Published in this edition 1993
© Gyldenal Norsk Forlag A/S 1963
English translation © Peter Owen and Elizabeth Rokkan 1966, 1993

ISBN 0–7206–0881–3

A catalogue record for this book is available
from the British Library.

Printed and made in Great Britain.

Part One

SISS AND UNN

I

Siss

A young, white forehead boring through the darkness. An eleven-year-old girl. Siss.

It was really only afternoon, but already dark. A hard frost in late autumn. Stars, but no moon, and no snow to give a glimmer of light—so the darkness was thick, in spite of the stars. On each side was the forest, deathly still, with everything that might be alive and shivering in there at that moment.

Siss thought about many things as she walked, bundled up against the frost. She was on her way to Unn, a girl she scarcely knew, for the first time; on her way to something unfamiliar, which was why it was exciting.

She gave a start. A loud noise had interrupted her thoughts, her expectancy; a noise like a long-drawn out crack, moving further and further off, while the sound died away. It was from the ice on the big lake down below. And it was nothing dangerous, in fact it was good news : the noise meant that the ice was a little bit stronger. It thundered like gunshot, blasting long fissures, narrow as a knife-blade, from the surface down into the depths— yet the ice was stronger and safer each morning. There had been an unusually long period of severe frost this autumn.

Biting cold. But Siss was not afraid of the *cold*. It wasn't

7

that. She had started at the noise in the dark, but then she stepped out steadily along the road.

The way to Unn was not long. Siss was familiar with it, it was almost the same as the way she went to school, only with the addition of a side path. That was why she had been allowed to go alone, even though it was no longer light. Father and Mother were not nervous about things like that. It's the main road, they had said when she left this evening. She let them say it. She was afraid of the dark herself.

The main road. All the same it was no fun to be walking down it alone now. Her forehead was boldly erect because of it. Her heart thumped slightly against the warm lining of her coat. Her ears were alert—because it was much too quiet along the roadsides, and because she knew that even more alert ears were there, listening to her.

That was why she had to step out firmly and steadily on the stone-hard road: the clatter of her footsteps had to be heard. If she gave way to the temptation to go on tiptoe, she was finished, let alone if she foolishly began to run. Then she would soon be running in panic.

Siss had to go to see Unn this evening. And she should have plenty of time, considering how long the evenings were. The darkness came so early that Siss could stay with Unn for a good while and still be home by her usual bedtime.

Wonder what I shall find out at Unn's. I'm sure to find out something. I've been waiting for it all the autumn, ever since the first day Unn came new to school. I don't know why.

The idea of meeting each other was so completely new, it had only come about that very day. After long preparation they had dived in head first.

On her way to Unn, quivering with expectancy. Her smooth forehead breached an ice-cold stream.

2

Unn

On her way towards something exciting . . . Siss thought about what she knew of Unn, as she walked stiff and erect, trying to shut out her fear of the dark.

She did not know much. And it would have been no use asking people here; they were not likely to be able to tell her more about Unn.

Unn was so new here. She had come to the district last spring, from another district quite far away, so there had been no communication between the two. She had come last spring after she had been orphaned, it had been said. Her mother had been taken ill and died, somewhere in their home district. She had been unmarried, with no close relatives there, but here in this district she had an older sister, so Unn had come to her aunt.

Her aunt had been here for a long time. Siss scarcely knew her, although she lived quite close. She kept house all alone in a little cottage, managing as best she could. She was seldom seen, except on her way to the store. Siss had heard it said that Unn had been made very welcome in her house. Siss had gone there with her mother once; Mother had needed help with some sewing. That had been several years ago, before she had known of Unn's existence. Siss could remember a lonely person sitting there, full of good nature. Nobody ever spoke ill of her.

It had been the same with Unn when she came : she had not joined the group of girls straightaway, as they had expected and hoped. They caught sight of her on the road and at other places where one could not help but meet people. They looked at each other like strangers. There was nothing to be done about it. She had no parents, and it put her in a different light, an aura they could not quite explain. They knew too that this strange situation would soon be ended : in the autumn they would meet at school—and that would be the end of that.

Siss had made no move to approach Unn during the summer either. She had seen Unn now and again, together with her kind old aunt; had met her and noticed that they were about the same height. They looked at each other in astonishment and brushed past. They did not know why they were astonished, but for some reason or other—

Unn was shy, it was said. It sounded exciting. All the girls had looked forward to meeting Unn, who was shy, at school.

Siss looked forward to it for a special reason : she was the acknowledged leader in their noisy breaks. She was used to being the one who made suggestions; she had never thought it over, it was so, and she did not dislike it. She had looked forward to being the leader when Unn arrived and had to be taken up.

When school started the class gathered as usual round Siss, the boys as well as the girls. She knew she was enjoying it this year too, and perhaps made an effort to keep her position.

Unn was standing shyly a short distance away. They

looked at her critically, and accepted her at once. There didn't seem to be anything the matter with *her*. An attractive girl. Likeable.

But she stayed where she was. They made small attempts to entice her to them, but it was no use. Siss stood in the middle of her group waiting for her, and the first day went by.

Several days went by. Unn made no sign of approach. Finally Siss went across to her and asked, ' Aren't you going to join us?'

Unn replied with a shake of the head.

But they were quick to see that they liked each other. A curious look flashed between them : *I must meet her!* Perplexing, but beyond doubt.

Siss repeated in astonishment, ' You're not going to join us?'

Unn smiled in embarrassment. ' No.'

' But why not?'

Unn still smiled in embarrassment. ' I can't.'

At the same time it seemed to Siss that they were both playing some game of enticement.

' What's the matter with you?' asked Siss bluntly and stupidly, and regretted it at once. Unn did not look as if there was anything the matter with her. On the contrary.

Unn flushed. ' No, it's not that, but—'

' No, I didn't mean it like that either. But it would have been fun to have you with us.'

' Don't ask me about it any more,' said Unn.

Siss felt as if cold water had been thrown on her, leaving her speechless. Mortified, she went back to her companions and told them.

So they did not ask Unn again. She was left to stand

alone, taking no part in their games. Some of them said she was conceited, but it did not gain currency, and nobody teased her—there was something about her that put a stop to anything like that.

In class it was immediately apparent that Unn was one of the brightest. But she did not put on airs and they acquired a grudging respect for her.

Siss took note of it all. She sensed that Unn was strong in her lonely position in the school-yard, not lost and pathetic. Siss used her power to win over the group, and was successful; all the same she had the feeling that Unn over there was the stronger, even though she did nothing and had no support. She was losing to Unn, and perhaps the group saw it this way too? It was just that they dared not go over. Unn and Siss stood there like two combatants, but it was a silent struggle, a matter between herself and the newcomer. It was not even hinted at.

After a while Siss began to feel Unn's eyes on her in class. Unn sat a couple of desks behind her, so she had plenty of opportunity.

Siss felt it as a peculiar tingling in her body. She liked it so much she scarcely bothered to hide it. She pretended not to notice, but felt herself to be enmeshed in something strange and pleasant. These were not searching or envious eyes; there was desire in them—when she was quick enough to meet them. There was expectancy. Unn pretended indifference as soon as they were out of doors, and made no approach. But from time to time Siss would notice the sweet tingling in her body : Unn is sitting looking at me.

She saw to it that she almost never met those eyes. She did not yet dare to do so—only in a few swift snatches when she forgot.

13

But what does Unn want?

Some day she'll tell me.

Out of doors Unn stood by the wall without taking part in any of their games. She stood watching them calmly.

Wait. Better wait, and it would be sure to come some day. For the time being she must be content with things as they were, and they were strange enough.

She must never let the others notice anything. And she thought she had managed it. Then one of her friends said to her, a little enviously. 'You *are* interested in Unn, I must say.'

'No, I'm not.'

'Aren't you? You stare at her the whole time, do you think we don't notice?'

Do I? thought Siss, stunned.

Her friend laughed sourly. 'We all noticed it a long time ago, Siss.'

'All right, I have then, and I shall do it as much as I like!'

'Yah!'

Siss had thought about it all constantly. And then at last it had come, *now*. Now, today. That was why she was walking here.

Early this morning the first note had been lying on her desk : 'Must meet you, Siss.' Signed, 'Unn'.

A ray of light from somewhere.

She turned and met the eyes. They were at one with each other. Extraordinary. She knew no more than that, she could think no more about it.

Notes had crossed on this wonderful day. Willing hands helped them along from desk to desk.

'Would like to meet you too.' Signed, 'Siss'.

'*When* can I meet you?'

'Whenever you like, Unn. You can meet me today.'

'I'd like it to be today, then.'

'Will you come home with me today, Unn?'

'No. You must come home with me, or I shan't meet you.'

Siss turned round abruptly. What was this? She met the eyes, saw Unn's nod confirming the note. Siss did not hesitate for a second, but sent her reply : 'I'll come with you.'

And the notes ceased. They did not speak to each other until the school day was over. Then they stood talking quickly and shyly. Siss asked whether Unn would come home with her all the same?

'No, why should I?' asked Unn.

Siss hesitated. She knew it was because she thought she might have something that Unn's aunt did not have—and then she was used to her friends coming to her. She was ashamed and could not tell Unn this.

'No, nothing special,' she said.

'You've said you'll come to me now.'

'Yes, but I can't go with you straightaway. I must go home first, so they'll know where I am.'

'Yes, I suppose so.'

'Then I'll come this evening,' said Siss, fascinated. It was the mystification that fascinated her, the aura she seemed to see all round Unn.

This was what Siss knew about Unn—and now she was on her way to her, after going home to let them know.

The cold nibbled at her. It creaked underfoot, and the

ice thundered down below. Then she caught sight of the
little cottage where Unn and her aunt lived. Light shone
out on to the frosted birch trees. Her heart pounded in joy
and anticipation.

3

One Single Evening

Unn must have been standing at the window watching for Siss, for she came out before Siss reached the doorstep. She was wearing her school slacks.

' It must have been dark?' she asked.

'Dark? Yes, but that doesn't matter,' replied Siss, although she had been quite nervous of the darkness and the short cut through the wood.

' It must have been cold too? It's dreadfully cold here this evening.'

' That doesn't matter either,' said Siss.

Unn said: 'It's such fun that you wanted to come. Auntie says you've been here only once before, and then you were quite small.'

' Yes, I remember that. I didn't know about you then.'

They took stock of each other as they talked. Auntie came out, smiling pleasantly.

' This is Auntie,' said Unn.

'Good evening, Siss. Come along in quickly, it's too cold to stand out there. Come into the warm and take off your things.'

Unn's aunt was friendly and placid. They went into the warm little living-room. Siss took off her boots, which were frozen hard.

17

'Do you remember how it looked when you were here before?' asked Auntie.

'No.'

'It hasn't changed either, it's exactly the same as it was then. You were here with your mother. I remember it very well.'

Auntie seemed to be talkative; presumably she seldom got the chance to chat. Unn stood waiting until she could have her guest to herself. But her aunt was not ready yet.

'Since then I've seen you everywhere but here, Siss. Of course there was nothing to bring you here either—until Unn came to live with me. It makes such a difference. I'm lucky to have Unn, you know.'

Unn waited with impatience.

Auntie said: 'I know, Unn. But don't be in such a hurry. Now Siss must get something warm inside her.'

'I'm not cold.'

'It's all ready on the stove,' said Auntie. 'I think it's too cold and too late to be out at this time of day and in this weather. You ought to have come on a Sunday.'

Siss looked at Unn and replied, 'I couldn't do that when it *was* today.'

Auntie laughed good-naturedly. 'No, in that case . . .'

'And I'll get home easily before Mother and Father go to bed,' said Siss.

'Yes. Come over here and drink this.'

They drank what Auntie had made them. It was good, and warmed them. Siss's excitement lapped round her, subtle and enticing. Soon they would be left alone.

Unn said: 'I have my own room. We'll go there.'

Siss's tension snapped. Now it would begin.

18

'You have a room to yourself too, don't you, Siss?'
Siss nodded.
'Come on then.'
Auntie, so friendly and talkative, looked as if she wanted
to come with them into Unn's bedroom. She was clearly
not allowed to do so. Unn interrupted so decisively that
Auntie was left sitting in her chair.

Unn's room was tidy, and Siss immediately thought there
was something strange about it. Two small lamps made it
bright. All kinds of newspaper cuttings had been hung on
the walls, and a photograph of a woman so like Unn that
there was no need to ask who she was. After a while Siss
saw that the room was not at all strange; on the contrary
it was very like Siss's own.

Unn looked at her enquiringly. Siss said : 'It's a nice
room.'
'What's yours like? Is it bigger?'
'No, about the same.'
'There's no need to have anything bigger.'
'No, there isn't.'
They had to make small talk for a bit before they could
get going. Siss sat on the only chair, her trousered legs
stretched out in front of her. Unn sat on the edge of the
bed, swinging her legs in the air.

They pulled themselves together, looked at each other
searchingly, and took stock. This was not so simple—for
some mysterious reason. They were embarrassed as well
because they wanted each other's company. Their eyes
met in understanding, in a kind of longing, yet they were
deeply embarrassed.

Unn jumped down on to the floor and pulled at the door
handle. Then she turned the key.

19

Siss started at the sound and asked quickly, 'Why did you do that?'

'Oh, she might come in.'

'Are you scared of that?'

'Scared? Of course not. It's not that. But I want us two to be alone together. Nobody is to come in now!'

'No, nobody is to come in now,' repeated Siss, beginning to feel happy. She felt that the bond between Unn and herself was beginning to be tied. Back in their places they fell silent again. Then Unn asked : 'How old are you, Siss?'

'Eleven and a bit.'

'I'm eleven, too,' said Unn.

'We're about the same height.'

'Yes, we're almost the same size,' said Unn.

Even though they felt drawn to one another, it was difficult to get the conversation going. They sat fingering objects within reach, and looking about them. The room was snugly warm. It was on account of the roaring stove of course, but not that alone. A roaring stove would not have helped if they had not been attuned to one another.

In this warmth Siss asked : 'Do you like living here with us?'

'Yes, I like being with Auntie.'

'Yes, of course, that's not what I meant. I mean at school and—why do you never—?'

'Look, I said you weren't to ask me about that,' said Unn curtly, and Siss had already regretted the question.

'Are you going to stay here for good now?' she asked quickly—surely *that* couldn't be dangerous? Was there some danger here? No, there couldn't be, but she didn't feel quite safe either; evidently it was easy to go too far.

'Yes, I'm going to stay here,' answered Unn. 'I have nobody else to stay with now besides Auntie.'

They sat in silence again. Then Unn asked searchingly: 'Why don't you ask about my mother?'

'What?'

Siss looked away at the wall as if caught.

'Don't know,' she said.

She met Unn's eyes again. It was unavoidable. So was the question. It had to be answered because it was about something important. She stammered: 'Because she died last spring, I suppose. That's what I heard.'

Unn said clearly and loudly: 'My mother wasn't married either. That's why there's no—' She stopped.

Siss nodded.

Unn went on: 'Last spring she fell ill and died. She was ill for only one week. Then she died.'

'Yes.'

It was a relief when this had been said; the atmosphere felt lighter. The whole district knew what Unn had just told her: Auntie had said all this and more when Unn arrived last spring. Didn't Unn know that? Still, it had to be talked about now in this beginning of the friendship that was to be forged. There was something else too. Unn said: 'Do you know anything about my father?'

'No!'

'Nor do I, except for the little Mother told me. I've never seen him. He had a car.'

'Yes, I suppose he did.'

'Why should he?'

'Oh, I don't know—people often do have cars, don't they?'

'Yes, I suppose so. I've never seen him. There's nobody

else besides Auntie now. I shall stay with Auntie for ever.

Yes! thought Siss, Unn would stay here for ever. Unn had a clear pair of eyes that held Siss fascinated, just as they had done the very first time. There was no more talk about parents. Siss's father and mother were never mentioned. Siss was sure Unn knew everything about them; they were simply at home in a respectable house, Father had a respectable job, they had everything they needed and there was nothing she could tell her. Neither did Unn enquire. It was as if Siss had fewer parents than Unn.

But she did remember siblings.

'You have brothers and sisters, don't you, Siss?'

'No, there's only me.'

'That's very convenient then,' said Unn.

It occurred to Siss what Unn's remark really meant: she was going to stay here for ever. Their friendship lay open before them like a smooth path. Something important had happened.

'Of course it's convenient. It means we can meet even more often.'

'We meet every day at school as it is.'

'So we do.'

They laughed briefly at each other. This was easy. It was just as it should be. Unn took down a mirror that was hanging on the wall beside the bed and sat down again, holding it in her lap.

'Come over here.'

Siss did not know what this was about, but she sat beside Unn on the edge of the bed. They each held a corner of the mirror, held it up in front of them, and sat without moving, side by side, almost cheek to cheek.

What did they see?

Before they were even aware of it they were completely engrossed.

Four eyes full of gleams and radiance beneath their lashes, filling the looking-glass. Questions shooting out and then hiding again. I don't know: Gleams and radiance, gleaming from you to me, from me to you, and from me to you alone—into the mirror and out again, and never an answer about what this is, never an explanation. Those pouting red lips of yours, no they're mine, how alike! Hair done in the same way, and gleams and radiance. It's ourselves! We can do nothing about it, it's as if it comes from another world. The picture begins to waver, flows out to the edges, collects itself, no it doesn't. It's a mouth smiling. A mouth from another world. No, it isn't a mouth, it isn't a smile, nobody knows what it is—it's only eyelashes open wide above gleams and radiance.

They let the mirror fall, looked at each other with flushed faces, stunned. They shone towards each other, were one with each other; it was an incredible moment.

Siss asked : ' Unn, did you know about this?'

Unn asked : ' Did you see it too?'

At once things were awkward. Unn shook herself. They had to sit for a while and come to their senses after this strange event.

In a little while one of them said : ' I don't suppose it was anything.'

' No, I don't suppose it was.'

' But it was strange.'

Of course it was something, it had not gone, they were only trying to push it away. Unn replaced the mirror and sat down with apparent calm. Both of them kept silent and waited. Nobody tried the handle of the locked door. Auntie was leaving them in peace.

Apparent calm. Siss was watching Unn now, and she saw how Unn was controlling herself. Her heart gave a jump when Unn said abruptly, enticement in her voice : ' Siss, let's undress !'

Siss stared at her : ' Undress?'

Unn seemed to be glittering. ' Yes. Only undress. That's fun, isn't it?'

She began to do so at once.

Of course! Suddenly Siss too thought it would be fun, and began taking off her clothes in a rush, racing with Unn, to be ready before Unn.

Unn had the lead and was first. She stood shining on the floor.

Immediately afterwards Siss stood, shining too. They looked at each other. The briefest of strange moments.

Siss was on the point of making the sort of racket that presumably was expected of her, and looked about her for something to tackle. She got no further. She noticed Unn's quick glances, something tense in her face. Unn was standing very still. For a moment it was there, then it was gone. Unn's face was happier, easy and pleasant to look at.

At once she said, as if happy in a topsy-turvy way : ' Ugh no, Siss, it's cold after all. I think we'd better dress again at once.' She picked up her clothes.

Siss stayed where she was. ' Aren't we going to kick up a row?' She was ready to turn somersaults on the bed and perform similar antics.

' No, it's too cold. It doesn't get warm enough indoors when there's such a hard frost outside. Not in this house.

24

' But it is warm here, I think.'

' No, there's a draught. Can't you feel it too? When you stop to think about it?'

' Maybe.'

Siss thought about it. It was true. She was a bit cold. The window-pane was covered with rime. Out of doors there had been frost for an eternity. Siss snatched up her clothes as well.

' There are plenty of things to do besides running about naked,' said Unn.

' Of course there are.'

Siss wanted to ask Unn why she had done this, but found it difficult to begin. She let it go. They put their clothes on again without haste. To tell the truth, Siss somehow felt cheated. Was this all?

They sat in the same places as before, the only places there were in the little bedroom. Unn sat and looked at Siss, and Siss realized that there was something that had not come out after all. Perhaps it might become exciting. Unn did not look happy any more—what had happened just now had only been a flickering of the eyelids.

Siss became nervous.

' Aren't we going to find anything to do?' she asked when Unn failed to take action.

' What should we do?' said Unn abstractedly.

' If not I must go home.'

It sounded like a threat. Unn said quickly : ' You mustn't go home yet !'

Oh no, Siss didn't want to either. She was really trembling with eagerness to stay.

' Haven't you any pictures of where you lived before? Haven't you an album?'

It was a bulls-eye. Unn ran to the bookshelf and took out two albums.

'This one is all of me. Me all the time. Which one do you want to see?'

'Everything.'

They turned the pages. The pictures were of somewhere far away, and Siss did not recognize a soul, except when Unn was included. She was in most of them. Unn provided brief comments. It was like all other photograph albums. A radiant girl peeped out from the page. Unn said proudly: 'That's Mother.'

They looked at her for a long time.

'And that's Father,' said Unn a little later. An ordinary youth standing beside a car. He looked a little like Unn too.

'That's his car,' said Unn.

Siss asked, half afraid: 'Where is he now?'

Unn replied discouragingly: 'Don't know. It doesn't matter.'

'No.'

'I told you, I've never seen him. Only his picture.'

Siss nodded.

'If they'd been able to find Father, I don't suppose I'd have come to Auntie,' added Unn.

'No, of course not.'

Once more they looked through the album with just Unn in it. She had been a splendid girl all along, thought Siss. Then they came to the end of that too.

What next?

They were waiting for something. She could tell by Unn's silence. Siss had been waiting for it all the time, so tensely that she started twice as violently when it finally did come out. Now it came tumbling as if out of a sack. After a long silence Unn said : ' Siss.'

The start!

' Yes?'

' There's something I want—' said Unn, flushing. Siss was already embarrassed.

' Oh?'

' Did you see anything on me just now?' asked Unn quickly, but looking Siss straight in the eyes.

Siss became even more embarrassed. ' No!'

' There's something I want to tell you,' began Unn again, her voice unrecognizable.

Siss held her breath.

Unn did not continue. But then she said : ' I've *never* said it to anyone.'

Siss stammered : ' Would you have said it to your mother?'

' No!'

Silence.

Siss saw that Unn's eyes were full of anxiety. Was she not going to tell her? Siss asked, almost in a whisper : ' Will you say it now?'

Unn drew herself up : ' No.'

' All right.'

Again silence. They began to wish Auntie had come and tried the door.

Siss began : ' But if—'

' I can't, so there!'

Siss drew away. All kinds of notions raced pell-mell through her brain, and were rejected. She said helplessly : ' Was this what you wanted?'

Unn nodded. ' Yes, that was all.'

Unn nodded as if relieved, as if something was over and done with. There was nothing else to come. At once Siss felt relieved as well.

Relieved, but as if cheated too for the second time that evening. All the same, it was better than hearing something that might frighten her.

They sat for a while as if resting.

Siss thought : I'd like to go now.

Unn said : ' Don't go, Siss.'

Silence again.

But the silence was not to be trusted, nor had it been any of the time. Here the wind came in sudden, capricious gusts, quick to change direction. It had dropped, but here it was again, unexpectedly, making her jump.

' Siss.'

' Yes?'

' I'm not sure that I'll go to heaven.'

Unn looked away at the wall as she said this; it was impossible to look anywhere else. Siss went hot and cold : ' What?'

She must not stay here. Unn might make up her mind to say more.

Unn asked : ' You heard what I said?'

' Yes!' She added quickly : ' I must go home now.'

' Home?'

' Yes, or I'll be late. I must get home before they go to bed.'

' They won't go to bed yet.'

' I must go home, so there.' She hastened to add : ' Soon it'll be so cold my nose will drop off on the way.' She was forced to talk nonsense in her perplexity. Somehow she had to get out of this. She simply had to run away.

Then Unn giggled as she should at what Siss had said, readily joining in the joke.

'You mustn't do that,' she said, 'let your nose drop off,' glad because Siss had changed the subject. Again they felt they had avoided matters that were too difficult.

Unn turned the key in the lock. 'Sit down. I'm only going to fetch your clothes,' she said commandingly.

Siss was on tenterhooks now. It was unsafe here. What might not Unn say? But to be with Unn! For ever. She would say before they parted: You can tell me more another time. Whenever you like, another time. We couldn't have gone further this evening. It had been a great deal as it was. But if they were to go further it would make things impossible. Home again as quickly as she could.

Otherwise they might get involved in something that would shatter it all for them. Instead they had shone into each other's eyes.

Unn came with her coat and boots, and put them down beside the roaring stove. 'They might as well get warm.'

'No, I must go,' said Siss, already putting on her boots.

Unn stood without speaking while Siss bundled herself up against the frost. It was no use talking nonsense any more about her nose freezing off, they were tense again. They did not say the things that are usual in parting: Won't you come again soon? Won't you come to me next time? It did not occur to them. It was all embarrassing and difficult. Not spoiled in any way, but far too difficult just now, face to face.

Siss was ready.

'Why are you going?'

'I told you, I must go home.'

' Yes, but—'

' When I've *said* I must—'

' Siss—'

' Let me go.'

The door was unlocked now, but Unn was barring the way. They both went in to Auntie.

Auntie was sitting in her chair with some kind of handwork. She got to her feet, just as friendly as she had been earlier that evening.

' Well, Siss, are you leaving us already?'

' Yes, I think I ought to go home.'

' No secrets left?' she asked teasingly.

' Not this evening.'

' I heard you lock the door, Unn.'

' Yes, I did lock it.'

' Well, you can never be too careful,' said Auntie. ' Is anything the matter?' she asked in a different tone of voice.

' The matter? Of course not!'

' You're so cross?'

' We're not a bit cross!'

' All right, never mind. I suppose I'm getting old and hard of hearing.'

' Thank you for having me,' said Siss, trying to get away from Auntie who only teased them and made them look stupid and knew absolutely nothing at all.

' Wait a bit,' said Auntie. ' You must have something warm before you go out into the cold.'

' No thank you, not now.'

' You *are* in a hurry.'

' She has to go home,' said Unn.

' Very well.'

Siss drew herself up: 'Good-bye, and thank you very much for having me.'

'Thank you for coming, Siss. Now you must run to keep warm. I can see it's getting colder and colder. Black as pitch too.

'Why are you standing there, Unn?' insisted Auntie. 'You'll be seeing each other in the morning.'

'Yes, we shall!' said Siss. 'Good night.'

Unn stood in the doorway after Auntie had gone in. Just stood. What had happened to them? It felt as if it was almost impossible to part. Something strange had happened.

'Unn—'

'Yes.'

Siss jumped out into the cold. She could easily have stayed longer, she had plenty of time, but it was dangerous. Nothing more must happen.

Unn remained in the open doorway, where the cold and the warmth met. The cold moved past her into the living-room. Unn seemed not to notice.

Siss looked back before she began running. Unn was still standing in the lighted doorway, beautiful and strange and shy.

4
The Side of the Road

Siss ran home. At once she was struggling blindly with her fear of the dark.

It said : It is I at the sides of the road.

No, no ! She thought at random.

I'm coming, it said at the sides of the road.

She ran, knowing there was something at her heels, right behind her.

Who is it?

Straight from Unn and into this. Had she not known that the way home would be like this?

She had known, but she had had to go to Unn.

A noise somewhere down in the ice. It ran along the flat expanse and seemed to disappear into a hole. The thickening ice was playing at making mile-long cracks. Siss jumped at the sound.

Out of balance. She had not had anything safe with which to set out on the return journey through the darkness, no firm footsteps striding along the road, as she had when she walked *to* Unn. Thoughtlessly she had started running, and the damage was done. At once she had been abandoned to the unknown, who walks behind one's back on such evenings.

Full of the unknown.

Being with Unn had made her over-excited—even more so after she had said good-bye and left. She had been afraid when she took the first steps, half-running, and her fear had increased like an avalanche. She was in the hands of whatever it was at the sides of the road.

The darkness at the sides of the road. It possesses neither form nor name, but whoever passes here knows when it comes out and follows after and sends shudders like rippling streams down his back.

Siss was in the middle of it, understanding nothing, simply afraid of the dark.

I'll be home soon!

No you won't.

She did not even notice the frost tearing at her breath.

She tried to cling to the image of the living-room in the lamplight at home. Warm and bright. Mother and Father in their arm-chairs. Then their only child would come home, their only child who, they tell each other, must not be spoiled, whom they have turned into a game so as not to spoil her—no, it was no use, she was not *there*, she was between the things at the sides of the road.

But Unn?

She thought about Unn : splendid, beautiful, lonely Unn.

What's the matter with Unn?

She stiffened in mid-stride.

What's the matter with Unn?

She started once more. Something gave warning behind her back.

We are at the sides of the road.

Run!

Siss ran. There was a deep, powerful thunderclap somewhere in the ice on the lake, and her boots clattered on
the frozen road. There was some comfort in it; if you
couldn't hear the sound of your own footsteps you might
go crazy. She hadn't the strength to run very fast any more,
but went on running all the same.

At last she could see the light at home.

At last.

To come into the light of the outside lamp!

They fell back, the things at the sides of the road, and
once more turned into a mutter outside the circle of light,
leaving Siss to go in to Mother and Father. Father had an
office in the district, and now he was sitting comfortably
in his chair, very much at home. Mother was reading as she
usually did when she had time. It was not yet time for bed.

They did not jump up anxiously when they saw Siss, out
of breath and covered in rime. They sat in their chairs and
said calmly, ' What in the world, Siss?'

She stared at them at first. Weren't they afraid? No, not
in the least. No, of course not—it was only she who was
afraid, she who had come from outside. What in the world,
Siss? they said placidly. They knew she could come to no
harm. Nor could they say much less than, what in the
world—since she had come home gasping and exhausted,
her breath frozen into icicles on her upturned coat collar.

' Is anything the matter, Siss?'

She shook her head, ' I was only running.'

' Were you afraid of the dark?' they asked, laughing a
little, as one ought at people who are.

Siss said, ' Pooh, afraid!'

' Hm, I'm not so sure,' said Father. ' But in any case
you should be too big for that sort of thing now.'

'Yes, you look as if you've been running for dear life the whole way,' said Mother.

'Had to come home before you went to bed. After all, you did say—'

'You knew we shouldn't be going to bed for some time yet, so you needn't have—'

Siss was struggling with her frozen boots; she let them thud on to the floor.

'What a lot of remarks you're making this evening.'

'What remarks?' They looked at her in amazement. 'Have we said anything?'

Siss did not reply, but busied herself with her boots and socks.

Mother got up from her chair. 'It doesn't look as if you—' she began, but stopped. Something about Siss stopped her.

'Go in and have a wash first, Siss. It will make you feel better.'

'Yes, Mother.'

It did too. She took a long time over it. She knew she could not avoid being questioned. She came back again and found herself a chair, not daring to dive into her own bedroom. So there would be even more prying. She might as well face it.

Mother said : 'That's much better.'

Siss waited.

Mother said : 'What was it like at Unn's then, Siss? Was it fun?'

'It was nice !' said Siss sharply.

'Doesn't sound much like it,' said Father smiling at her.

Mother looked up too : 'What's the matter this evening?'

35

She looked at them. They were being as kind as they knew how, she supposed, but—

'Nothing,' she said. 'But you do pry so. Pry about everything.'

'Oh come, Siss.'

'Go in and get something to eat. It's standing on the kitchen table.'

'I've had something to eat.'

She had not, but serve them right.

'Very well, you'd better go to bed then. You look worn out. And I expect it'll be all right in the morning. Good night, Siss.'

'Good night.'

She went at once. They understood nothing. Once in bed she realized how tired she was. She had strange, upsetting things to think about, but the warmth after the cold stole up on her, and she did not think for long.

5

The Ice Palace

' Up you get, Unn !'

Auntie's usual call, today as on any other ordinary school day.

But for Unn it was no ordinary day, it was the morning after the meeting with Siss.

' Up you get, Unn !' though there was no hurry to get to school. But Auntie was like that, she never let you wait till the last minute.

Unn heard the usual thunderclap from the steel-hard ice out there in the darkness when she put her head out. It was like a signal that the new day had begun. But inside her room during the night she had heard a dull thud too, telling her, before she finally fell asleep, that now it was the very middle of the night. It had taken her a long time to get to sleep after the evening with Siss, thinking about everything that might *happen*, together with Siss.

It was colder than ever outside said Auntie, who was getting the breakfast. Unn looked at the hard, glittering stars above the house. You could barely see that the eastern sky was growing paler : a stark, wintry pre-Christmas dawn.

As the darkness thinned, trees appeared, white with rime; Unn watched them as she got ready for school.

For school and for Siss.

And she would not think about *the other* today !

37

At once it struck her how impossible it was to meet Siss again only a few hours after the awkward way in which they had parted. She had scared Siss so that Siss had run away. It was no use meeting her straight away! It was no use going to school today.

She looked out at the forest of rime-white trees in the brightening dawn. She would have to hide somewhere, get away, not meet Siss today.

Tomorrow it would be different, but not just *now*. She could not look into Siss's eyes today. She thought no further; the idea took hold of her with compelling force.

Siss, whom she was dying to meet, and yet—

In any case she would have to leave as she did every day. It was no use sitting down and saying that she didn't want to go to school. Auntie would never accept that. It was too late to say she was ill too—besides, she was not in the habit of making excuses. She looked at herself quickly in the mirror : she did not look the least bit ill, it was no use telling fibs. She would leave for school as usual, and then make off before she met anyone. Make off and hide until school was over.

Even though Auntie had called and woken her, she said, when Unn was ready with her satchel, 'Are you going *so* early?'

'Is it any earlier than usual?'

'I think so.'

'I want to meet Siss.' She felt a twinge as she said it.

'Oh, of course. Are you in such a hurry?'

'Mm.'

'Then it's no use my saying anything, I can see. Off you go. It's a blessing your coat's thick, it's bitterly cold. Put on two pairs of mitts too.'

Her words seemed like fences alongside the road to school; it was difficult to climb over them, and they led straight to school. But not today! Not after Siss had run away from her last night.

'What is it, Unn?'

Unn jerked herself back. 'Can't find my mitts.'

'Here. Right under your nose.'

She left the house in the fading darkness. She had to find out how to keep away today as soon as she was out of sight.

No, she had only one thought today : Siss.

This is the way to her. This is the way to Siss.

Can't meet her, only think about her.

Mustn't think about the other now, only about Siss whom I have found.

Siss and I in the mirror.

Gleams and radiance.

Only think about Siss.

With every step.

Now she was at the first rime-white tree that would hide her. There she left the road. She would have to keep hidden until she could come home again at the usual time without being questioned.

But what was she to do with herself? A whole long school day. And in such cold. The air she inhaled seemed to be trying to stop her breathing, to constrict it. It bit into her cheeks. But her warm coat, and being used to the cold this autumn, prevented her from feeling really chilled.

Boom! went the thunder in the black, shining steel on the frozen lake.

39

That was it! That was the solution. She knew at once what she would do: she would go to see the ice.

All by herself.

Then she would have plenty to do all day, and could keep warm and everything.

The trip to see the ice had been discussed at school during the past few days. Unn had not taken part in it, but had heard enough to know what it was all about, and that they would have to go very soon, for the snow might come any day now.

There was a waterfall some distance away that had built up an extraordinary mountain of ice around it during this long, hard period of cold. It was said to look like a palace, and nobody could remember it happening before. This palace was the purpose of the outing. First along the lake to the outlet, and then down the river to the waterfall. A short winter's day like this was just right for it.

Splendid, her day would be filled.

But I was going to see it with Siss!

She chased the thought away by thinking warmly and happily: I shall see it for the *second* time with Siss—that will be even better.

The ice on the lake shone so brightly that it did not look like ice at all. Steel-ice. Not a snowflake had fallen into the water when it froze, and not a snowflake had fallen since.

Now the ice was thick and safe. It thundered and cracked and hardened. Unn was running towards it. It seemed natural to run because of the cold. Besides, she was running in order to get quickly away from the part where people might be—since she was going to hide all day.

She had managed it now. The urgent call—'Unn, come here!' in Auntie's kind voice—did not come. Auntie thought she was at school now.

But what would they make of it at school? She hadn't thought about that.

That she was ill, for once. Of course. Would Siss think so too? Perhaps Siss would understand why.

Unn ran across the frozen, stone-hard ground which echoed her footsteps. The rimed trees stood with glades in between. She ran zig-zag between the trees so as to keep herself hidden from peering eyes. Only now would she go out on the ice and walk along the edge of the lake.

She thought about Siss. Their meeting tomorrow—when everything had evened itself out a little and was not so impossible as today. All of a sudden she was no longer alone. She had found someone to whom she could tell everything, soon.

She ran in joy towards the ice, across the frosted ground and between the rimed birch twigs; they glittered like silver. For now it was almost light. Pale stalks stuck up, rimed and bent, with pale, broad leaves—Unn knocked them over as she ran and the silver trickled dry as sand over her boots.

She thought with joy about the ice: thicker and thicker; that was how the ice should be.

It thundered at night. You would be awake, perhaps, and would think : still thicker.

The walls of the old log house cracked too in this cold. The timbers were shrinking, said Auntie. If you heard that at night it was no use saying thicker and thicker, you thought : Now it's terribly cold, it's thundering in the house.

She was at the lake shore now, and nobody seemed to have seen her, not the least glimpse so that they could tell anyone about her. The ice was deserted, as she had known it would be, so early in the day. Later in the morning the small fry would come; they were allowed to rough and tumble here as much as they liked, since the ice was as strong as rock without any dangerous or hidden rifts. The lake was big, it was an enormous expanse of ice.

It was fun looking through the black, shining ice close to the shore. Unn was not too grown-up to do so, lying flat on her stomach, her hands shielding her face to direct her gaze. It was like looking through a pane of glass.

Just then the sun rose, cold and slanting, and shone through the ice straight down to the brown bottom, with its mud and stones and weeds.

A little way out from the land the water was frozen solid. Even the bottom was white with rime and had the thick layer of steel-ice on top of it. Frozen into this block of ice were broad, sword-shaped leaves, thin straws, seeds and detritus from the woods, a brown, straddling ant—all mingled with bubbles that had formed and which appeared clearly as beads when the sun's rays reached them. Smooth, black, fresh-water stones from the lakeside were also transfixed in the block together with peeling sticks. Bent bracken stood in the ice like delicate drawings. Some were rooted in the bottom, some had been caught by the congealing water as they lay floating on the surface. Then the surface had stiffened and it had continued to build itself up.

Unn lay watching, captivated by it; it was stranger than any fairy story.

I must see more . . .

She lay flat on the ice, not yet feeling the cold. Her slim body was a shadow with distorted human form down on the bottom.

Then she changed her position on the shining glass mirror. The delicate bracken still stood in the block of ice in a blaze of light.

There was the terrifying drop.

Where it was deeper, the bottom and everything else were brown. Among the few weeds a small, black shellfish lay in the mud, moving one of its feet. Nothing came of it; it did not stir out of the slime or alter its position. But immediately beyond it the wall of mud plunged down almost sheer into a totally black chasm.

The terrifying drop.

Unn moved, and the gliding shadow followed her, fell right across the chasm and disappeared as if sucked down so quickly that Unn flinched. Then she understood.

Her body quivered a little as she lay there; it looked as if she were lying in the clear water. Unn felt a fleeting dizziness, and then realized afresh that she was lying safely on top of thick, steel-hard ice.

It was uncomfortable looking at the sheer drop all the same. It meant certain death for anyone unable to swim. Unn could swim now, but there had been a time when she could not, and one day she had gone over just such a fall. She had been wading—when suddenly there was nothing beneath her foot. She went rigid, knowing that she was just about to—but then a rough hand had snatched

43

her back on to safe ground, back to her noisy companions.

Unn did not finish her train of thought about the horrid drop—a streak of light came from the darkness and up towards her : a fish moving as fast as an arrow, as if making straight for her eyes. She shrank aside, forgetting that there was ice between them. There was a stripe of grey-green back, then a jerk to one side and the flick of a glassy eye looking to see what she was.

That was all, down again into the depths.

And she knew very well what the little fish had wanted. Now he was down there already, telling the others, she imagined. In a way she liked it.

But the inquisitive fish had cut across the bond that kept her tied to the spot. She was cold too. She got up and began half running, sliding on the slippery ice. Some of the time she was on land, running quickly across headlands that jutted out into the lake, then out on the ice again. It made her warm, and it was fun.

She did this for a long time; it was some distance to the outlet. But at last she arrived.

She neither saw nor heard the waterfall, it was lower down. Here there was merely a whisper of water as it travelled downwards, and up at the outlet it was quite still and noiseless.

This was the outlet of the great lake : a placid sliding of water from under the edge of the ice, so smooth that it was scarcely possible to see it. But a veil of vapour rose up from it in the cold. She was not conscious that she was standing looking at it; it was like being in a good dream. A good dream could be made out of so simple a thing. She felt no pangs of conscience because she was out on a walk

44

without permission, and it would perhaps be difficult to find excuses for it. The placid water flowing away from the ice filled her with quiet joy.

She would probably lose her hold and fall down into a hollow where the shadows were, this time too, but it was a good moment and the other was chased away again by the sight that streamed towards her : the great river coming noiseless and clear from under the ice, flowing through her and lifting her up and saying something to her which was just what she needed.

They were so still, she and the water, that now she thought she heard the waterfall, the distant roar where this sliding water threw itself over the precipice. You were not supposed to be able to hear the falls from here, she knew that from school. Now she could just hear it.

That was where she was going. And she would *not* think about the other. She would be free of it today !

All of them would be going down there on the school outing. The roar came like a faint echo through the frosty air, and really she should not have been hearing it.

Supple and black and without a sound the lake slid forward from under the polished edge of the ice, new and clean all the time, and as placid as if sliding in a dream.

The distant tremor of the falls reminded her of where she was going. She awoke. She would have liked to tell somebody what she was feeling now—but she would never manage it, she knew.

She realized how cold she was as soon as she stood still. The frost bored through her clothes. She began running to get warm.

Just below the outlet the ground began to slope a little. The noiseless water began to whisper. The sloping river banks were a tracery of curious ice formations, after all the frosty weather and the spray from the warmer stream of water. The river crept in among them and licked at the icicles.

The ground was made up of heather and tussocks of grass and, like everything else, shone silver with rime in the slanting sunlight. Unn jumped from tussock to tussock in this fairyland. Inside her satchel her books and sandwich box jumped up and down too.

The slope became steeper. At once the stream began making more noise, between protruding black river stones wearing shining crowns of ice. Unn was running here without permission. She thought : I didn't really want to either. But the truth was that she wanted to more and more.

Now she could distinctly hear the enticing roar below. Continually flowing away—and the more enticing it was, the more right it was.

Her impetuous running had made her warm. Her breath lay in small clouds about her whenever she paused. Her thick coat was too stiff for hurrying in. Unn was warm right through, and her eyes were glittering. At intervals she paused on the tussocks and made lots of clouds with her warm, healthy breath.

It became steeper, the river surged more loudly, but the roar of the falls still remained in the background, threatening and enticingly low. She thought as if in defiance : I didn't want to do this !

But she did. It had to do with Siss.

It was the only thing that was right, even though it was disobedient and wrong. She could never turn back now. It had to do with Siss and all the good things she could glimpse from now on. If she were to turn away from this,

46

if she were to retreat from the roar down there and return home empty-handed, she would feel a chasm of deprivation, a longing for something she would never find again.

The roar was suddenly stronger. The river began to quicken its speed, flowing in yellow channels. Unn ran down the slope alongside, in a silvered confusion of heather and grass tussocks, an occasional tree among them. The roar was stronger, thick whorls of spray rose up abruptly in front of her—she was at the top of the falls.

She stopped short as if about to fall over the edge, so abruptly did it appear.

Two waves went through her : first the paralysing cold, then the reviving warmth—as happens on great occasions.

Unn was there for the first time. No one had asked her to come here with them during the summer. Auntie had mentioned that there was a waterfall, no more. There had been no discussion of it until now, in the late autumn at school, after the ice palace had come and was worth seeing.

And what was this?

It must be the ice palace.

The sun had suddenly disappeared. There was a ravine with steep sides; the sun would perhaps reach into it later, but now it was in ice-cold shadow. Unn looked down into an enchanted world of small pinnacles, gables, frosted domes, soft curves and confused tracery. All of it was ice, and the water spurted between, building it up continually. Branches of the waterfall had been diverted and rushed into new channels, creating new forms. Everything shone. The sun had not yet come, but it shone ice-blue and green of itself, and deathly cold. The waterfall plunged into the middle of it as if diving into a black cellar. Up on the edge of the rock the water spread out in stripes, the colour changing from black to green, from green to yellow and white, as the fall became wilder. A booming came from the cellar-hole where the water dashed itself into white foam against the stones on the bottom. Huge puffs of mist rose into the air.

Unn began to shout for joy. It was drowned in the surge and din, just as her warm clouds of breath were swallowed up by the cold spume.

The spume and the spray at each side did not stop for an instant, but went on building minutely and surely, though frenziedly. The water was taken out of its course to build with the help of the frost: larger, taller, alcoves and passages and alleyways, and domes of ice above them; far more intricate and splendid than anything Unn had even seen before.

She was looking right down on it. She had to see it from below, and she began to climb down the steep, rimed slope at the side of the waterfall. She was completely absorbed by the palace, so stupendous did it appear to her.

Only when she was down at the foot of it did she see it as a little girl on the ground would see it, and every scrap of guilty conscience vanished. She could not help thinking that nothing had been more right than to go there. The enormous ice palace proved to be seven times bigger and more extravagant from this angle.

From here the ice walls seemed to touch the sky; they grew as she thought about them. She was intoxicated. The place was full of wings and turrets, how many it was impossible to say. The water had made it swell in all directions, and the main waterfall plunged down in the middle, keeping a space clear for itself.

48

There were places that the water had abandoned, so that they were completed, shining and dry. Others were covered in spume and water drops, and trickling moisture that in a flash turned into blue-green ice.

It was an enchanted palace. She must try to find a way in! It was bound to be full of curious passages and doorways—and she must get in. It looked so extraordinary that Unn forgot everything else as she stood in front of it. She was aware of nothing but her desire to enter.

But finding the way was not so simple. Many places that looked like openings cheated her, but she did not give up, and so she found a fissure with water trickling through it, wide enough to squeeze herself through.

Unn's heart was thudding as she entered the first room. Green, with shafts of subdued light penetrating here and there; empty but for the biting cold. There was something sinister about the room.

Without thinking she shouted 'Hey!', calling for someone. The emptiness had that effect; you had to shout in it. She did not know why, she knew there was nobody there.

The reply came at once. 'Hey!' answered the room weakly.

How she started!

One might have expected the room to be as quiet as the tomb, but it was filled with an even roaring. The noise of the waterfall penetrated the mass of ice. The wild play of the water outside, dashing itself to foam against the stones on the bottom, was a low, dangerous churning in here.

Unn stood for a little to let her fright ebb away. She did not know what she had called to and did not know what had answered her. It could not have been an ordinary echo.

Perhaps the room was not so large after all? It felt

large. She did not try to see whether she could get more answers, instead she looked for a way out, a means of getting further in. It did not occur to her for a moment to squeeze out into the daylight again.

And she found a way as soon as she looked for it: a large fissure between polished columns of ice.

She emerged into a room that was more like a passage, but was a room all the same. She tested it with a half-whispered 'Hey!' and got a half-frightened 'Hey!' back again. She knew that rooms like this belonged in palaces—she was bewitched and ensnared, and let what had been lie behind her. At this moment she thought only of palaces.

She did not shout 'Siss!' in the dark passage, she shouted 'Hey!' She did not think about Siss in this unexpected enchantment, she thought about room upon room in a green ice palace, and that she must enter each one of them.

The cold was piercing, and she tried to see whether she could make big clouds with her breath, but the light was too dim. Here the noise of the waterfall came from below —but that couldn't be right? Nothing was right in such a palace, but you seemed to accept it.

She had to admit she was a little chilled and shivering, in spite of the warm coat Auntie had given her when the wintry weather had set in this autumn. But she would soon forget about it in the excitement of the next room, and the room was to be found, as surely as she was Unn.

As might be expected in a narrow room, there was a way out at the other end: green, dry ice, a fissure abandoned by the water.

When she arrived inside the next one she caught her breath at what she saw: she was in the middle of a petrified forest. An ice forest.

50

The water, which had spurted up here for a while, had fashioned stems and branches of rice, and small trees stuck up from the bottom among the large ones. There were things here too that could not be described as either the one or the other—but they belonged to such a place and one had to accept everything as it came. She stared wide-eyed into a strange fairy-tale. The water was roaring far away.

The room was light. No sunshine—it was probably still behind the hill—but the daylight sidled in, glimmering curiously through the ice walls. It was dreadfully cold.

But the cold was of no importance as long as she was there; that was how it should be, this was the home of the cold. Unn looked round-eyed at the forest, and here too she gave a faltering and tentative shout: 'Hey!'

There was no reply.

She started in surprise. It didn't answer!

Everything was stone-hard ice. Everything was unusual. But it did not answer, and that was not right. She shuddered, and felt herself to be in danger.

The forest was hostile. The room was magnificent beyond belief, but it was hostile and it frightened her. She looked for a way out at once, before anything should happen. Forward or back meant nothing to her any longer; she had lost all sense of it.

And she found another fissure to squeeze through. They seemed to open up for her wherever she went. When she was through she was met by a new kind of light that she was to recognize from her past life: it was ordinary day-light.

She looked about her hastily, a little disappointed; it was the ordinary sky above her! No ceiling of ice, but a cold blue winter sky reassuringly high up. She was in a round room with smooth walls of ice. The water had been here, but had been channelled elsewhere afterwards.

Unn did not dare to shout 'Hey!' here. The ice forest had put a stop to that, but she stood and tested her clouds of breath in this ordinary light. She felt colder and colder when she remembered to think about it. The warmth from her walk had been used up long ago, the warmth inside her was now in these small clouds of breath. She let them rise up in quick succession.

She was about to go on, but stopped abruptly. Someone had called 'Hey!' From *that* direction. She spun round and found no one. But she had not imagined it.

She supposed that if the visitor did not call, then the room did so. She was not sure she liked it, but answered with a soft 'Hey!' really no more than a whisper.

But it made her feel better. She seemed to have done the right thing, so she took courage from it and looked round for a fissure so that she could go on at once. The roar of the falling water was loud and deep at this point; she was close to it without being able to see it. She must go on!

Unn was shivering with cold now, but she did not know it, she was much too excited. There was the opening! As soon as she wanted one it was there.

Through it quickly.

But this was unexpected too : she was standing in what looked like a room of tears.

As soon as she stepped in she felt a trickling drop on the back of her neck. The opening she had come through was so low that she had had to bend double.

It was a room of tears. The light in the glass walls was

very weak, and the whole room seemed to trickle and weep with these falling drops in the half dark. Nothing had been built up there yet, the drops fell from the roof with a soft splash, down into each little pool of tears. It was all very sad.

They fell into her coat and her woollen cap. It didn't matter, but her heart was heavy as lead. It was weeping. What was it weeping for?

It must stop!

It did not stop. On the contrary, it seemed to increase. The water was coming in this direction in greater quantities, the trickling went faster, the tears fell copiously.

It began oozing down the walls. She felt as if her heart would break.

Unn knew well enough that it was water, but it was a room of tears just the same. It made her sadder and sadder : it was no use calling anyone or being called in a room like this. She did not even notice the roar of the water.

The drops turned to ice on her coat. In deep distress she tried to leave. She stumbled along the walls, and at once she found the way out—or the way in, for all she knew.

A way out which was narrower than any of the others through which she had squeezed, but which looked as if it led into a brightly lit hall. Unn could just see it, and she was wild with the desire to enter it; it seemed to be a matter of life and death.

Too narrow, she could not get through. But she had to get in. It's the thick coat, she thought, and tore off coat and satchel, leaving them to lie there until she came back. She did not think much about that, in any case, only about getting in.

And now she managed it, slender and supple as she was, when she pushed hard enough.

The new room was a miracle, it seemed to her. The light shone strong and green through the walls and the ceiling, raising her spirits after their drenching in the tears.

Of course! Suddenly she understood, now she could see it clearly: it had been herself crying so hard in there. She did not know why, but it had been herself, plunged in her own tears.

It was nothing to bother about. It had just been a pause in the doorway as she had stepped into this clean-swept room, luminous with green light. Not a drop on the ceiling here, and the roar of the waterfall was muffled. This room seemed to be made for shouting in, if you had something to shout about, a wild shout about companionship and comfort.

It gushed out, she called ' Siss!'

When she had done so she started. ' Siss!' came in answer from at least three directions.

She stood still until the shout mingled with the roar. Then she crossed the room. As she did so she thought about her mother, and about Siss, and about the other—she managed it for a very brief moment. The call had made an opening; now it slammed shut again.

Why am I here? It occurred to her, as she walked up and down. Not so many steps, she was walking more and more stiffly and unrecognizably. Why am I here? She attempted to find the solution to this riddle. Meanwhile she walked, strangely exalted, half unconscious.

She was close to the edge now : the ice laid its hand upon her.

She sensed the paralysing frost. Her coat had been left somewhere else, that was the reason. Now the cold could bore into her body as it liked. She felt herself getting frightened, and darted across to the wall to get out to her warm coat. Where had she come in?

The wall was a mountain of ice, compact and smooth. She darted across to another. How many walls were there? All was compact and smooth wherever she turned. She began shouting childishly, ' I must get out!' Immediately she found the opening.

But this palace was odd : she did not get back to her coat, she came out into something she did not like very much.

Yet another room. It was really tiny, and full of dripping icicles hanging down from the low ceiling, full of icicles growing up from the floor, and jagged walls with many angles, so thick that the green light was deadened. But the roar of the waterfall was not deadened, here it was suddenly very close, or underneath, or wherever it might be —it was like being right *inside* it.

The water trickled down the walls of this room, reminding her of the one in which she had cried. She did not cry now. The cold prevented that and blurred everything. Much was flashing through her mind, but as if in a mist; if she tried to grasp it, something else was there instead. It must have occurred to her that surely this was dangerous, she would shout loudly and challengingly the shout that was part of the ice palace : ' Hey! Hey!'

But it could scarcely be called a proper shout. Another thought laid itself across it, and she barely heard it herself.

It did not carry at all; the only answer was the savage roar. The roar swept all other sounds away. Nor did it matter. Another thought, and another ray of cold had already chopped it off.

It occurred to her that the roar was like something to lie down in, just to lie down in and be carried away. As far as you wanted—no, that one was chopped off.

The floor was wet with the drops. In some places the surface of the water was freezing thinly. *This* was no place to be—Unn searched the complicated walls yet again for an opening.

This was the last room; she could go no further.

She thought this only vaguely. At any rate there was no way out. This time it was no use, whatever she did. There were plenty of fissures, but they did not lead out to anything, only further in to ice and strange flashes of light.

But she had come in, after all?

No use thinking like that. It was not in, it was out now —and that was another matter, she thought confusedly. The fissure through which she had entered was naturally not to be found when she wanted to leave again.

No use calling, the roar drowned it. A hollow of tears was ready waiting in front of her. She could plunge into it, but she could not drag herself so far. She had finished with that elsewhere.

Was someone knocking on the wall?

No, nobody would knock on the wall here! You don't knock on walls of ice. What she was looking for was a dry patch to stand on.

At last she found a corner where there was no moisture, but dry frost. There she sat down with her feet tucked under her, her feet, which she could no longer feel.

Now the cold began to stiffen her whole body, and she no longer felt it so keenly. She felt tired, and had to sit down for a while before she began looking seriously for the way out and an escape—away from here—out to her coat and out to Auntie and out to Siss.

Her thoughts became gradually more confused and vague. She distinguished Mother for a while, then she slid away too. And all the rest was a mist, threaded with flashes, but not so as to hold her attention. There would be time enough to think about it later.

Everything was so long ago, it receded. She was tired of all this running about in the palace, in all this strangeness, so it was good to sit for a while, now that the cold was not troubling her so much. She sat squeezing her hands together hard. She had forgotten why. After all, she was wearing her double mitts.

The drops began to play to her. At first she had heard nothing besides the tremendous roar, but now she could distinguish the plim-plam of the falling drops. They oozed out of the low ceiling and fell on to icicles and into puddles —and there was a song in it, monotonous and incessant: plim-plam, plim-plam.

And what was *that*?

She straightened up. Something was flooding over her that she had never felt before, she began to shout—now she had a deep, black well of shouts if she should need them—but she did not let out more than one.

There was something in the ice! At first it had no form, but the moment she shouted it took shape, and shone out like an eye of ice up there, confronting her, putting a stop to her thoughts.

57

It was clearly an eye, a tremendous eye.

It grew wider and wider as it looked at her, right in the middle of the ice, and full of light. That was why she had shouted only once. And yet when she looked again it was not frightening.

Her thoughts were simple now. The cold had paralysed them little by little. The eye in the ice was big and looked at her unblinkingly, but there was no need to be afraid, all she thought was : What are you looking for? Here I am. More hazily a familiar thought in such situations came to her : I haven't done anything.

No need to be afraid.

She settled down again as before, with her feet drawn up, and looked about her, for the eye was bringing more light, the room was more distinct.

It's only a big eye.

There *are* big eyes here.

But she felt it looking at her from up there, and she was obliged to raise her head and meet the eye without flinching.

Here I am. I've been here all the time. I haven't done anything.

Gradually the room filled with the plim-plam of the water drops. Each drop was like a fraction of a song. Beneath played the harsh, incessant roar, and then came the high plim-plam, like more pleasant music in the middle of it. It reminded her of something she had forgotten a long time ago, and because of that it was familiar and reassuring.

The light increased.

The eye confronted her, giving out more light. But Unn

58

looked at it boldly, letting it widen as much as it would, letting it inspect her as closely as it wished; she was not afraid of it.

She was not cold either. She was not comfortable, she was strangely paralysed, but she did not feel cold. Hazily she remembered a time when it had been dreadfully cold in the palace, but not now. She felt quite heavy and limp, she really would have liked to sleep for a little, but the eye kept her awake.

Now she no longer stirred, but sat against the wall with her head raised so that she could look straight at the light in the ice. The light became increasingly brighter and began to fill up with fire. Between herself and the eye were the quick glints of the falling drops as they made their monotonous music.

The fiery eye had been merely a warning, for now the room was suddenly drowned in flame. The winter sun was at last high enough to enter the ice palace.

The late, cold sun retained a surprising amount of its strength. Its rays penetrated thick ice walls and corners and fissures, and broke the light into wonderful patterns and colours, making the sad room dance. The icicles hanging from the ceiling and the ones growing up from the floor, and the water drops themselves all danced together in the flood of light that broke in. And the drops shone and hardened and shone and hardened, making one drop the less each time in the little room. It would soon be filled.

A blinding flood of light. Unn had lost all ties with everything but light. The staring eye had burned up, everything was light. She thought dully that there was an awful lot of it.

She was ready for sleep, she was even warm as well. It

was not cold in here at any rate. The pattern in the ice wall danced in the room, the light shone more strongly. Everything that should have been upright was upside down —everything was piercingly bright. Not once did she think this was strange; it was just as it should be. She wanted to sleep; she was languid and limp and ready.

Part Two

SNOW-COVERED BRIDGES

I

Unn Vanishes

Was it only a strange dream? *Was* it Unn and me yesterday evening? Yes!

When her uncertainty had been dispelled the truth was clear : it had happened. In astonishment and joy.

Today all she felt was renewed longing for Unn. She must go straight to school to meet her. She could do it today, now things had changed.

Siss had to lie for a while thinking about all that was going to be new from now on. She made herself feel solemn by thinking : I am Unn's friend for ever. She made it as precious as she could.

Mother and Father asked her no questions today. Not a word about her rather unusual homecoming the night before. They would probably wait for a bit. For one day or two. Then they would ask as if inadvertently. That was how they managed to find out about most things.

But not this! This was the limit. Not a word about Unn would they get out of her. Whatever it was shining in Unn's eyes was much too delicate to be talked about.

The morning was like any other morning. Siss dressed herself warmly against the cold, took her satchel and set off for school.

Who would get there first? Unn's path did not join hers

63

until just before they reached school. They had never seen each other on the way there.

Will Unn be embarrassed today? she thought.

The frost felt keener than ever. The sky above the delicate silken twilight shimmered blue as steel. Today there was nothing frightening at the sides of the road; the morning darkness was pleasant as it dispersed, gradually and surely. Strange that one could get into a panic about it at night.

What is the matter with Unn?

She'll probably tell me again some time. I shan't think about it. I just want to be with her. She needn't tell me. It's something that hurts; I don't want to know what it is.

Unn had not arrived when Siss hurried into the warm classroom. Several of the others were there. Some of them said casually, 'Hi, Siss.'

She did not say a word about yesterday's meeting. They probably expected it, because of the exchange of notes, but they contained themselves. They were probably waiting to see what would happen when Unn turned up. Siss had it all worked out: as soon as Unn appeared in the doorway she would go to meet her so that everyone should see how things stood. The idea made her so happy that she tingled all over.

Had she altered already? A girl from the old group asked straight out, 'What's the matter, Siss?'

'Nothing.'

Could they already see that she would leave them and go to Unn as if rejoicing? Were their eyes *so* sharp? Oh well, it made no difference. In any case it would soon be no secret. In spite of awkwardness she would have to do it: go to Unn shining with friendliness.

Wasn't she going to come soon out of the twilight? Like something new?

There was no sign of her. Soon nearly all of them had come except Unn. The teacher came. Time was up.

The teacher said good morning.

But wasn't Unn coming?

It was immediately verified from the charge desk: 'Unn's missing today.'

They began the lesson.

Unn's missing today. A calm statement of fact. Siss, who was watchful, thought she heard slight surprise in the teacher's voice. Others would certainly have heard nothing. Sometimes one of them was missing, sometimes another. No fuss was made. It was noted in a thick register that Unn had not come to school today. That was all.

Siss sat nervously at her desk.

She had noticed that Unn never played truant from school, so it must have been something special today. And Siss connected it without hesitation with their meeting in her bedroom yesterday evening. Did Unn simply not want to meet her today? Was she *so* embarrassed?

In the break Siss tried to behave as usual. Nobody said she didn't, so she must have succeeded. Nor did anybody mention Unn, who was missing; she was an outsider after all.

The school day proceeded. The late winter sun rose and shone as best it could on the window panes. Siss simply waited for the sun to go down and the day to end, so that she could get away and ask after Unn. The day felt long.

Shortly after noon the sun went in. Before it began its

65

brief downward course it became veiled in mist, a mist that soon turned into thick, grey cloud.

Up at the charge desk the voice was saying : 'The weather report said there'd be a change this afternoon. They're expecting snow.'

Snow.

The first time this year.

Brief, but full of meaning : snow.

It had a special ring. Everyone in the room was so very well aware of what the word stood for : an important part of life. Snow.

The voice up there continued : 'So the cold weather will probably break too.'

And again : 'But then the snow will cover the ice.'

For a moment each one of them thought of something sad : funerals or something similar. That was what it sounded like. The lake was black and shining like steel for the last time. There had been a cold, but marvellous skating season for a long time. Today it would end, today the snow would come.

When they went out of doors after the next lesson the ice had already begun to whiten.

Here in the schoolyard the ground was still bare, but the air was grey and you could feel a few invisible flakes on your face if you lifted it. The enormous expanse of ice was already white. The flat surface of the mirror had no resistance, collecting the snowflakes long before anything else.

Extraordinary how quickly a thing can be destroyed. The ice was flat and white and dead.

And then it came at last, when they were called in to the next lesson : 'Does anyone know why Unn isn't here today?'

66

Nobody could have seen the start it gave Siss. It was over already. They looked at each other; nobody indicated that they knew anything.

' No,' came the reply finally, in all sincerity.

' I've been half expecting her to come all day,' the teacher said. ' It's not like her. But I suppose she must be ill.'

They realized that Unn was of more importance than they had normally reckoned. Perhaps they had always known. They must have heard how bright she could be. But she stood over there keeping out of things. On the rare occasions when she did join in she would break off as soon as it was over, and then she would stand there just as before, looking superior or whatever it was.

They looked innocently up at the charge desk. They realized that Unn was being praised. The teacher looked up and down the rows : ' Isn't there anybody who's friends with Unn and knows whether she might be ill? She hasn't stayed away for a single day all the autumn.'

Nobody replied. Siss sat on tenterhooks.

' Is she *so* lonely?' asked the teacher.

' No, she's not !'

Everyone turned towards Siss. It was she who had said, or almost shouted it. She sat scarlet at her desk.

' Was that you, Siss?'

' Yes, it was.'

' Do you know Unn?'

' Yes?'

The others looked sceptical.

' Well, do you know what's the matter with her today?'

' I haven't seen her today.'

Siss looked so unlike her usual self that the teacher felt

67

he should go into this more than he had intended. He came over to her. 'You said that—'

'I said that I'm Unn's friend,' burst out Siss before he had time to finish. Now they know, she thought.

One of the girls sitting near her looked as if she wanted to ask: Since when? So she added defiantly, 'I was her friend yesterday evening. So now you know!'

'My dear child!' said the teacher. 'What have we done, Siss?'

'Nothing.'

'So Unn was all right yesterday evening?'

'Yes, she was.'

'I see. Well, in that case perhaps you'd call in on her on the way home and find out what's the matter. I know she comes to school a different way, but you don't mind the extra walk, do you?'

'No,' said Siss.

'Thank you.'

The others looked at Siss in astonishment, and asked in the last break: 'What do you know about Unn?'

'Don't know anything.'

'We don't believe that. We can see you know something. The teacher could see it too.'

They were rather cross. They were unable to swallow the fact that Siss seemed to have gone over to Unn all of a sudden. They could tell she knew something she didn't want to talk about.

'We can see you know, Siss.'

She looked back at them helplessly. Suddenly there existed some extraordinary thing about Unn which only Siss knew.

They were on their way home. Above them the sky thickened. As yet there was only a sprinkling of snow. Siss went on ahead with several of the others. She could see that they were thinking. What does she know about Unn? They came to the place where Siss had to turn off the road. They all came to a halt, in an odd way. They were offended. Siss was to blame.

' What is it?' she asked sharply.

They let her go.

She hurried as quickly as she could down the path to the litle cottage. Then—there it came : the snow.

The snow was released. The air had turned mild now that darkness was falling; now real snow could come. It showered down over a frozen landscape. Hard earth and frozen hillsides. It happened just before Siss reached Auntie's house. When she got there the yard was already white.

Not a soul to be seen.

What do I know about Unn?

They think there is something. There is, too, but *it's* for *Unn and me*. And perhaps for God, she added, to be on the safe side, staring out into the driving snow.

An important little pause on the way.

Through the driving snow she saw Auntie come out as soon as she entered the yard. Whatever did that mean? Now she realized that she was uneasy in advance—and there was Auntie coming out as if she had been on the watch for her. Why should she be doing that?

Siss took several big leaps through the sifting snow—the first to set foot in the fresh carpet. Auntie waited, small and lonely, looking sad through the tattered snowflakes.

'Has something happened to Unn?' she half shouted before Siss reached the doorstep.

'What?' gasped Siss.

This puzzling little knocking.

She had to turn everything round. It had been standing on its head.

'I asked why you've come, and not Unn?'

So all she could do was release the horror : 'But surely Unn's at home, isn't she?'

At once the dark shutters flew gaping wide. Flustered questions on both sides. A hasty search of house and woodshed to no purpose.

Flustered running. No telephone in the house, but there was one not far away. Auntie left to phone round.

'It will be dark before we can do anything,' she said as she began running.

Siss ran home to Mother and Father. Now she needed them, needed anything they might say. The snow sifted down and the first darkness began to appear.

Again Siss ran along the road. Now in the fresh snow it seemed dazzlingly new. She met no cars, there were no tracks. She did not think about the sides of the road, only about coming home, giving warning.

2

Vigil

Unn has vanished.

It's getting dark.

It mustn't!

But the early darkness would not be delayed by hap-hazard, desperate wishes; it continued to fill up and thicken rapidly.

People had now been warned over a wide area and had gathered to make a search. There were too few lanterns, and the evening and the driving snow turned the search into flustered confusion. Lantern-light and prolonged shouts for Unn were drowned in snow and the growing darkness. People walked in lines—and a wall of night confronted them. They intended to break the wall down. They did not give up either, and broke it down as best they could.

Unn had vanished.

If only this snow had come yesterday, said the searchers, there would have been tracks. Now it has come just too late and made matters worse.

Siss was part of the tumult. Nobody bothered about her to begin with. She ran with a lump in her throat. There had been a hard struggle at home before she was given permission.

71

' I *am* going, Father !'

' We're not having youngsters rushing about in the night and the storm,' said her father as he hurriedly got himself ready.

She had continued to threaten.

Then came an obvious question.

' What happened when you were with Unn yesterday evening, anything in particular?'

' No,' said Siss flatly.

' Yes, what did she say?' asked Mother, joining in. ' You did seem a bit odd when you came home. What did she say?'

' I shan't tell you !' said Siss, and was to regret it bitterly. She realized she had already said too much. It was pounced on in mid-air.

' Good heavens, did she say something so you know why this has happened?'

' No, I know *nothing* about it, so there !'

It was lucky they asked questions backwards, so that she could say no with a clear conscience. I ran away when Unn wanted to tell me, she thought.

Mother came up and said, ' I think she'd better go with you. We don't know what this is all about. You see how upset she is.'

So Siss went with them. At first several of her classmates shared in the confusion, but they were sent home. Siss kept to the edge of the crowd so that she would only be seen in glimpses.

Soon it was night. They were prepared to search all night through, if necessary. Unn must not be left lying out of doors.

Where should they search? Everywhere. There was

nothing to guide them. Auntie's house was the centre. Auntie herself was exhausted. A few of the men had just looked in to ask for advice : guessing here and guessing there.

'Up in the lake,' said somebody.

'Up in the lake? The only open water is near the big river. Surely she can't have gone that way?'

'What would she be doing there?'

'What would she be doing anywhere?'

'I can't help thinking of the road. The cars driven by all sorts of people.'

They were hushed and embarrassed, in this muttering from man to man, from which helpful people went out into the night and found nothing. The road. The eternally unsafe and open road. They preferred not to think about it.

'We've been telephoning for a long time in all directions,' said somebody hurriedly about the road.

'But there's something else; what about the waterfall, the big pile of ice that has built up there? There's supposed to have been some talk of a school trip to it. Could Unn have gone there on her own, and then got lost?'

Auntie interrupted. 'But to play truant from school to do that? That's not like Unn.'

'What would be like her, then?'

'Has she any friends?'

'No, none. She's not like that. Yesterday one of the girls was here for the first time since Unn came to live with me.'

'Oh? Yesterday? Who was that?'

'That one there, Siss. But she can't tell anything to-day. I've asked her. Though there was something she didn't

73

want to say. Something they were giggling about, I expect. I could see it when Siss went home last night. But *that's* not important.'

Auntie stood exhausted in the snow outside her house, completely useless as a guide. But she was still the centre.

'Why did the snow come *afterwards*?' she said. 'Immediately afterwards.'

'That's what always happens,' answered somebody despondently.

'No,' said Auntie.

Lights shone in all the houses that night. The new snow was trodden underfoot along all the paths and in between them. Lanterns winked, half blinded by the driving snow, in thickets and on the open heath. Shouts rose up, but did not reach far, unable to penetrate the pitch darkness.

'There'll be more chance of finding something in the morning when it gets light,' suggested somebody. But they could not possibly wait until then.

Siss had collapsed in a clump of trees. She was never at any time far enough away to be unable to see the lights and hear the noise. Her father was in touch with her to a certain extent, but she kept well to the edge. Suddenly she collapsed among the trees at the thought of Unn.

Where is Unn?

'Hey there!' called somebody close by, but she paid no attention, there was so much shouting.

She had collapsed. Not from fatigue, but from a different kind of helplessness.

Nothing must happen to Unn.

She heard steps behind her. She turned her head and

74

saw a young man in the rays of the lantern he was carrying; saw his face, and the joy in it shining warmly towards her: 'Hey there!'

She only cringed at the sound of his voice. But now he had reached her.

'No, you don't!' he said. 'I know what you're thinking. You're not going to run away from me!'

A pair of strong arms encircled her, she felt them hugging her hard in uncontrolled joy.

'I was certain I'd find you—I felt I would.'

She understood.

'But it's not me!'

He laughed.

'Try to get me to believe that. But I must say I think you're carrying this too far.'

'I tell you it's not me! I'm helping to look for Unn too.'

'Aren't you Unn?' said the stranger, his joy extinguished.

It sounded so wonderful, but she had to say, 'No, I'm Siss.'

The strong arms released her so suddenly that she fell against a stake and bruised herself. The boy said angrily: 'You'd better stop fooling around here like this. Everyone will think it's you.'

'I *must* come with you, so there. I know her. I know Unn.'

'Oh, do you?' he said more gently.

She was not angry with him either.

'Did you hurt yourself?'

'No, not a bit.'

'I didn't mean to—but I could see you did hurt yourself.'

A small joy in the midst of misery.

'But you mustn't fool people like that, when you're a little girl exactly like the one we're trying to find. We're not here for fun. You must go home at once,' he said, and began to be stern again.

Siss was defiant. They weren't going to talk to her as if she were an unwelcome child they wanted out of the way. She said thoughtlessly : ' I'm the only one who knows Unn. We were together yesterday evening.'

Was he impressed by that? No. He asked directly, half reluctantly, ' Do you know anything, then?'

She looked at him. The lantern was between them so that they could see each other's eyes clearly. His round eyes looked down and he went away.

Siss was to regret such thoughtless words. The atmosphere was tense. In a trice, she was caught in a net of her own making. It was reported quick as a flash that the little girl Siss knew something.

The minutes were precious. Before long a forceful hand was holding her arm. But this was no strange boy with kind eyes like marbles, it was the stony face of a man she knew, a face that was stony and frightening tonight, though not normally so.

' Is that you, Siss? You must come with me.'

Siss was numb.

' What do you want?'

' You ought to go home. You're not allowed to run about here like this. But there's something else too,' he said, making her tremble.

His hand was rough, she was forced to go with him.

' My father gave me permission, you know nothing about it,' she said defiantly. ' And I'm *not* tired.'

76

'Now then, come along. Some of us want to talk to you a bit.'

No! she thought.

The man let her go when they reached two other searchers—she knew them too. They came from the next district. She already knew what this meant.

'Where's Father?' she asked to brace herself.

'Oh, he's not very far away, I'll warrant. Now listen to me, Siss. You've said you know something about Unn. You were with her yesterday evening, you said.'

'Yes, I was. I was at her home for a while.'

'What did Unn talk about?'

'Oh—'

'What is it you know about Unn?'

Three pairs of eyes watched her sternly in the lantern light. Normally they were friendly; now they were afraid and hard as stone.

She did not answer.

'You must answer. It might save Unn's life.'

Siss started. 'No!'

'You've said you know something about Unn, haven't you?'

'She didn't say it. She didn't say anything about this.'

'What do you mean, this?'

'That she wanted to go anywhere.'

'Unn may have said something that could help us to look for her.'

'No, it couldn't.'

'What did Unn tell you?'

'Nothing.'

'Do you understand that this is serious? We're not

77

asking you to plague you, we're asking you in order to find Unn. You've said that—'

' It was only something I said!'

' I don't think so. I can see you know something. *What did Unn say?*'

' I can't tell you.'

' Why not?'

' Because it wasn't like that, she didn't *say* it! And she didn't say a word about hiding.'

' Maybe not, but all the same—'

She began to scream, ' Let me alone!'

They stopped abruptly. It sounded too risky when Siss screamed like that.

' Go home then, Siss. You're exhausted. I expect your mother's there.'

' I'm not tired. I've been given permission to stay. I *must* stay.'

' Must you?'

' Yes, I think I must.'

' We can't waste time on this. It's a pity you won't tell us anything. It might have helped us.'

No, she thought. They left her.

Her head felt empty and strange. There was an easy way home, but she had to stay all night. She wandered about as before, near the lanterns and then into the darkness that hid her once more. Again she was stopped, by a different man. He expressed no surprise at her presence; he was too preoccupied.

' There you are, Siss. I want to ask you something. Do you think Unn might have wanted to go and look at the pile of ice in the waterfall?'

' Don't know.'

78

'Weren't there plans for the whole school to go on such a trip?'

'Yes, there were.'

'She didn't mention that she wanted to go there by herself? She's in the habit of being by herself, you know.'

'She didn't say so.'

This couldn't have been so important, the man was exceedingly cautious, but for Siss it was the last straw. She stood howling, bitter and defiant, in the driving snow.

'Oh Lord,' said the man. 'I didn't mean to make you cry.'

'*Are* you going there?' Siss managed to get out.

'Yes, we must, and without any delay. Since there's been talk of it recently at school. It's *possible*,' he said, 'that Unn has taken it into her head to go there, and then lost her way. We shall go along the river, from the point where it leaves the lake.'

'But then—'

'Thank you for helping us, Siss. Hadn't you better go home now?'

'No, I'm coming with you to the river!'

'No fear! Well, you must talk to your father about that. I think I can see him over there.'

Yes, there was Father, energetic and stern, like the others.

'I want to come too. You said I could.'

'Not any more.'

'I'm just as good a walker as they are!' she said loudly in the busy, tense crowd—and felt her own body tensing itself in readiness.

'I bet she is,' said someone who liked to see her standing there warm and eager.

Father dared not oppose her, the way Siss looked at that moment.

'Well, well, it may be true that you can hold out. I shall have to go in somewhere and phone your mother. She's sitting up, waiting for you.'

A large crowd set off in the darkness to the river, out along the edge of the lake towards the outlet. They fanned outwards as they walked, but were careful to keep together. The snow was not falling so heavily now, but it sifted against the face incessantly, and already lay so deep on the ground that it made walking difficult. Siss did not notice it; she was filled with fresh courage.

Nearly all of them had lanterns. They formed a huge, wavering patch of light that flickered and shone over hillocks and headlands on its way to the river. It was a strange sight, it was strange to be walking in the middle of it. Siss was filled with fresh courage.

The lake curved away into the night like a white snow-covered plain. The ice was as strong as granite, so nothing could have happened there. They could not imagine that Unn would have crossed that stark expanse of ice.

They floundered along. Siss kept close to her father now that she had been accepted.

They came to the outlet, and directed the light on to the open, black water gliding gently from under the edge of the ice and on without a sound. The men studied the black water closely; it was horrid. They could not see the ice palace from here. The waterfall was much further down, out of earshot in all the confusion.

The current flowed deep and noiseless. The crowd divided and continued along each side.

The snow was falling more thickly again. It was a nuisance, sifting against the glass of the lanterns, where it melted, making their glow unreliable. There was a young boy who was over-excited and nervous about it all, and he snarled at the irritating snow, his teeth showing white at the corners of his mouth : ' Stop it !'

At once it stopped. It stopped as if the sack had suddenly emptied. The boy started and, feeling embarrassed, looked round quickly to see if anyone had noticed. No.

Now that the snow no longer filled the air—now the men saw for the first time what an enormous, silent night it was. Siss stood beside the noiseless current coming from under the edge of the ice. Anything could be hidden and sucked away down there. Don't think about it.

They began to walk downwards along the banks of the river, along beaches and inland among the hillocks. The land sloped, the river found its voice.

Hurry! They rushed across sticks and stones. But they had to look carefully at the same time.

The turbulent, leaping procession of lanterns kept company across the river, twinkling in the hard ice tracery edging it. In between them the water was black. The glimmer from the lanterns did not reach very far. Out there was the deep unknown. Far below they could just hear the waterfall.

There was nothing to be seen along the river banks.

We expected that, but still—that's how it is with searching.

A shout from the first to climb down : ' Come and look !'

At once they all saw it. At once Siss saw it. None of the men had had time for a walk to the falls that had been talked about so much this autumn, and the ice palace had grown so much only recently. Throughout the period of frost the water had gradually acquired a larger surface on which to build. The men raised their lanterns towards the sculptured waterfall, thunderstruck by what they saw.

Siss looked at them, at the palace, the darkness and the lanterns—she would never forget this expedition.

The crowd descended the slope on both sides of the waterfall, crawling out on to the uneven ice, shining their lanterns into all the crannies they could find.

The palace was twice as big in this uncertain light. The falls were high, and the water had built up from the ground to the very top. The men shone their lanterns on to the sheer, glistening sides. They were hard and closed; the snow had found no foothold but was piled up at the bottom. Up on top, however, the snow lay and provided a covering for the clefts between the pinnacles and domes. The lantern light wavered only a short way up the sides; further up the ice walls were grey in the darkness. Deep inside, like a menacing beast, the self-enclosed river roared.

But the palace was dark and dead; no light came from within. The men could not see how it looked inside the rooms; their lights did not reach far enough. All the same, the searchers were bewitched.

The water roared within the palace, dashed itself into froth against the rock beneath and emerged again as froth and spray, from under towers and walls, reassembled and was the same mighty current as before, hurrying on. In this densely-packed midnight it seemed impossible to guess how far.

Nothing to be seen except the palace and the river and immensity.

The palace was closed.

Siss looked to see whether the men were disappointed. No. They showed nothing. And, after all, it depended on what each of them expected to find. Everything depended on precisely that.

But the men just stood.

How has this actually been made?

Nobody was bothering about Siss now. They left her to accompany her father, and brought her no questions. They simply went on with the search. Nobody could have penetrated further into the mass of ice than they did. They converged from both sides in the snow on top of the domes and shouted advice to each other against the roar of the falls.

A shout came : 'There's an opening here after all!'

They hurried to the spot. It was an entry almost hidden between green walls. Two of the smallest forced their way in, holding a lantern high.

Nothing there either. Only an icy breath, much colder than it was outside, that chilled them to the marrow. Outside it was mild now. An ice chamber, and no more openings to be found. Behind it churned the blind, eternal roar.

They shouted to each other in the roaring chamber that there was nothing there! Then they shone the light round it once more, and found a fissure smaller than a hand's breadth, and with water gurgling at the edges.

Nothing.

They squeezed out again to the others. 'Nothing,' they reported.

'Might have expected it.'

The men looked helplessly at the construction of ice rising rampant into the air. Their faces were grave that night. The one who had assumed the leadership said : ' We shan't be through with this in a hurry.'

They could not guess the extent of his meaning. They must have sensed the enigma here, each one of them. Siss looked at her father. He had not attempted to lead them, he was simply one of the rest.

But someone in the crowd unexpectedly went over to Siss. She was a little tired, yes, very tired really, but so tense that she had forgotten about it. She looked in fear at the man : there would be more questions.

' Did Unn say anything about coming here?'

' No.'

Her father came up and said sharply, ' That's enough now ! Siss is not to be pressed any more.'

The leader came too, and said quickly and decisively to the questioner, ' Siss has told us what she knows.'

' I think so too,' said her father.

' I'm sorry,' said the questioner, retreating. ' I meant no harm.'

Siss gave the two stern men a grateful look. The leader said : ' We'll go over it all once more. There are so many chasms she could have fallen into—if she came here, and decided to climb.'

Nobody denied it. They set to work. The unfamiliar ice palace exerted a tremendous fascination, and *they* were the right ones to be open to it and to allow themselves to be bound by it, in their state of mind.

Over it again.

Once more Siss stood at the foot and watched the ice palace coming alive. The men approached it from all sides again. The lanterns spun round in the disordered crannies, up between the pinnacles and through the tracery. It was not just a palace; it resembled a palace illumined for a feast, even though the lights were on the outside.

Siss drank in the night scene, in a state of exaltation, because she had been allowed to come, in a state of shock because it was on account of Unn. She cried a little, but nobody saw; she could not help herself.

She was going to hold out whatever happened, she thought. They were not going home again from here. From the palace they would follow the river to the place where it was swallowed up by another frozen lake. It was not so very far; the waterfall lay almost exactly between the two big lakes.

The men continued to search. They had life and light on their side. They were visiting an unknown fortress, and it looked like the fortress of death. If one of them struck the wall with his stick it proved to be as hard as rock. The blow recoiled and vibrated in his arm. Nothing opened up. They struck all the same.

3

Before the Men Leave

They are not leaving, they are waiting. They cannot free themselves.

The ice construction rises above them, enigmatic, powerful, its pinnacles disappearing into the darkness and the winter cloud drift. It seems prepared to stand eternally— but time is misleadingly brief, it will fall one day when the floods begin.

Tonight it holds the men fast. They are staying longer than they ought, considering their errand. Perhaps they are unaware of it. They are tired out but cannot make an end of it, with no will to choose whether they are to finish or not. The closed ice palace has life in it.

They themselves have lent it life; light and life to the dead block of ice, and to the silent time that follows midnight. Before they came the waterfall had been roaring, despondent and unconcerned, and the colossus of ice had been merely death, completed and mute. They did not know what they had brought with them before they were ensnared by the play between what has been and what is to come.

But it's not that either.

There is something secret here. They bring out what sorrows they may have and transfer them to this midnight play of light and suspicion of death. It makes things better, and through it they fool themselves into enchantment. They are dispersed in the angles of ice, the lanterns shoot transverse gleams, meeting the lights from other cracks and prisms—quite new beams are illuminated, and just as quickly extinguished again for good. They recognize it so well that they tremble. It is unsafe, but they wish to do it, they have to take part in it. If there is an opening it is only because there appears to be one.

The men are forced to leave, but they do so reluctantly.

The men are lost in the game at the ice palace. They seem possessed, searching feverishly for something precious that has come to grief, yet involved themselves. They are tired, grave men, giving themselves over as sacrifices to an enchantment, saying: It is *here*. They stand at the foot of the ice walls with tense faces, ready to break into a song of mourning before the closed, compelling palace. If one of them had been impetuous enough to begin, all of them would have joined in.

Siss, the young girl, stands watching them open-mouthed, and realizes that there *is* something. She sees that they are ready to join in. She sees her father standing ready; he would have joined in. Siss would have stood shivering and listened, waiting for the walls to fall asunder. She stands appalled at grown men.

But there is no one impetuous enough, so the song does not begin. They are loyal searchers; they manage to keep their secret thoughts under lock and key.

The leader says: 'Go over it once more.' He is caught up in it himself, and could do unexpected things. They know time is precious. Laboriously they climb on the slippery ice and the snow-covered roof, finding nothing. The

water, with its hidden depths, slides away from under the
palace and onward. They too must go on. The leader says :
' We must go.' He too could have joined in the heart-
rending song.

4
Fever

Unn was standing in the doorway, looking in.

But wasn't Unn lost?

No. Unn was standing in the doorway, looking in.

'Siss?'

'Yes? Why don't you come in?'

She nodded and entered the room.

'What is it, Siss?' she asked, but in a different voice. She changed, and was not Unn, but Mother.

Siss was lying in bed in her little room, but everything else was vague. She saw Unn and then it was Mother. She was tossing about in a mist.

'You're not well, Siss. You have high fever.'

Mother spoke in her patient tone of voice.

'It was too much for you out in the woods last night,' she explained. 'You came home ill, you see.'

'But Unn?'

'Unn hasn't been found, as far as I know. They're out searching. And you came home ill early this morning.'

'Then I was with them all night!'

'Yes, you were, but you weren't up to it.'

'We were at the big pile of ice and down by the river too—but then I don't remember any more.'

'No, you weren't up to much when your father brought

you home. At least you managed to walk somehow. Then
the doctor came and—'

Siss interrupted. 'What's the time now? Is it evening?'

'Yes, it's evening again.'

'And Father? Where is he?'

'Out with the search party.'

He must be stronger than I am after all, thought Siss,
pleased with the idea.

'The rest of the class have been out today too,' continued
Mother. 'The school's been closed.'

That sounded strange. Closed. It had been closed. She
lay playing with it.

'It was so like Unn standing in the doorway. I don't
think she can be far away.'

'None of us can tell. But she wasn't in the doorway.
You've been seeing a lot of things today. You've been talking about them, at any rate.'

What did that mean? At once she felt naked and pulled
the bed-clothes up higher.

'What have I been doing?'

She had to cover it up somehow, had to start talking
about something.

'Unn isn't dead!'

Her mother answered patiently, 'No, I'm sure she isn't.
They'll find her soon. They may have found her already.'
She looked tentatively at Siss: 'And if there's anything
you . . .'

Siss fell asleep as fast as she could.

But after a while she really did sleep. When she awoke
the fever must have improved. She saw nothing in the
bedroom except what ought to have been there. She

roused herself a little—and at the first sound her mother came in again.

'You've been asleep for a long time. It's late in the evening. A deep, quiet sleep.'

'Late in the evening? Where's Father?'

'Out searching.'

'Is there no news?'

'No. They've found nothing, and no one can give them any guidance. Her aunt knows nothing. They don't know what to do, Siss.'

Here it was again, the thing that would destroy her. She was in its hands, defenceless. She knew nothing that could be of any help.

'Father came in just now while you were asleep. He wanted to ask you about something, but we didn't want to wake you. It was important, he said.'

Her mother can have had no idea how near the breaking point she was.

'Do you hear me, Siss?'

It was no use going to sleep again now. What have I said without knowing it? *Have* I said anything?

'Siss, try to remember what you and Unn really did talk about. What she said to you.'

Siss lay gripping the blanket, feeling the approach of something unfamiliar. Her mother continued: 'That was what Father said he had to know. Not just Father, but all of them searching want to know if you can give them some hint.'

'I told you, it was nothing!'

'But are you sure, Siss? While you were feverish you said a good deal that goes against you. You talked about the strangest things.'

Siss stared at her in fear.

'It's better for you to tell us. I don't want to threaten you, but it's important. All this is being done for Unn's sake.'

Siss felt the unfamiliar thing just above her, felt it take hold of her.

'But when I say I can't tell you anything, I can't do more, can I?'

'Siss—'

At once everything began to go dark, at once everything seemed strange and sinister. Her mother hurried to her. Siss shouted, 'She didn't say it, I tell you!' And the darkness was complete.

Her mother stood appalled and tried to rouse Siss. Siss lay contorted and wailing.

'Siss, we shan't do anything to you! . . . Do you hear? . . . Siss, I didn't know . . .'

5

In Deepest Snow

Then where was Unn?

A reply seemed to say, Snow. Blindly and meaninglessly.

Blindly all the long day. It was no longer cold, but it snowed unceasingly. Then came the evening, and with it the urgent question : Where is Unn?

Snow, came the reply from hearth and home. It was real winter. And Unn had vanished into it. In spite of all their searching, not a trace was to be found. It was as blind around Unn as in the blinding snowstorms.

People had not given up; there was some form of search taking place continually. But it was no use wading about the woods in the deep drifts. They kept watch and investigated in other ways.

In a trice everyone knew about Unn, the unknown Unn. There had been pictures in the newspapers; people had seen an enquiring photograph of her taken that summer.

The great lake was a silent expanse, no longer detonating, non-existent. The splendid broad outlet, where the water flowed placidly between softly rounded banks, was still there, but no one went there any more. Somewhere further along the hidden ice palace stood too, losing its

93

shape below the rising drifts. No one ploughed his way there, his skis sinking deep into the snow.

But the one night there in front of the ice walls had fixed itself in people's memories, and had turned into a legend about Unn: they were certain that Unn had climbed up there, fallen into the river and been carried away.

They were still dragging the river, downwards from the waterfall where there were pools. The ice-coated dragging poles stood in the snowdrifts at night, pointing upwards. All roads led to Auntie's house. Everything collected there, all lines of communication met in this lonely woman, Unn's sole anchor. The blind lanes crossed there at a clear, tearless point of intersection.

' I see,' said Auntie.

' Thank you,' she said. ' It can't be helped.'

Unn's anchor in life.

An enquiring picture taken last summer. Unn, eleven years old. It was at Auntie's, standing on the table.

She was given reports by those who had taken their turn with the dragging that day. Their poles stood outside while the tired men recounted their day to Auntie, who was always cordial. Others looked in at daybreak the next morning. It had snowed all night. It would be a winter with plenty of snow.

Auntie listened to the reports from the second, larger group, the one that was trying to find out whether Unn was still alive. There was no news.

' I see. Very well. Thank you very much.'

She also had to receive people who looked in to question her about everything that might throw light on the matter.

She had no information to guide them. They found an elderly, cordial woman. There must have been a great difference in age between her and Unn's mother. They looked at the picture that everyone had seen.

' It was taken last summer, wasn't it?'

Auntie nodded. She was tired of this.

The expression *taken last summer* had made the picture compelling from the very first. It was meaningless, but it had happened. It was impossible to guess what kind of enchantment the face was given by it, but it had gained something. Taken last summer. They looked at it and would not forget it.

They looked enquiringly at Auntie too, who was forced to submit to all this. She did not look very strong; but they realized that she was immensely strong in her imperturbability.

She had to answer one question which was unavoidable : ' What was Unn like?'

' I was very fond of her.'

That was all.

Those who heard this testimony from Auntie herself felt it was the finest that could be given. It bore no trace of the many times it had been said. They felt they had to look at the picture a little longer.

' She looks so enquiring, in a way, doesn't she?'

' Yes, what of it?'

What of it? Nothing.

' She lost her mother in the spring. She was all that she had. So she had something to enquire about, don't you think?'

Outside the window the snow fell, blotting out all traces.

6

The Promise

Promise in deepest snow from Siss to Unn :
I promise to think about no one but you.
To think about everything I know about you. To think
about you at home and at school, and on the way to school.
To think about you all day long, and if I wake up at
night.

Promise at night.
I feel you are so close that I could touch you, but I
daren't.
I feel you looking at me when I lie here in the dark. I
remember it all and I promise only to think about *that*, at
school tomorrow.
There is no one else.
I shall do so every day, as long as you are gone.

Solemn promise one winter's morning :
I feel you standing in the passage, waiting for me when
I go out. What are you thinking about?
I promise you it shan't happen again, what happened
yesterday. It wasn't important! There's still no one but
you.
No one, no one else.

You must believe me when I tell you so, Unn.

Renewal of the promise from Siss to Unn :
There is no one else. I shall never forget what I have promised, as long as you are gone.

7

Unn Cannot Be Blotted Out

So Unn could not be blotted out. This was something that came about in Siss's bedroom. There the dearly-bought promise took shape.

After a week she was able to get up. A week of driving snow against the window panes and many wakeful hours at night, with the knowledge that it was snowing harder than ever—because everything about Unn had to be snowed under. Blotted out. It was to be emphasized that she had gone for good, that it was useless to search.

Then resistance rose up strong and shining. Then the promises took shape. They took shape too when she heard how the reports from the search parties petered out; when it all seemed futile.

She won't be lost. She shan't be lost. Siss determined it in her room.

Nobody came to bother her with questions any more. Somebody had put a stop to that. She dreaded going to see Auntie; she would have to go as soon as she got up, it was the very first thing she must do.

If they had perhaps expected Auntie to come here to question Siss then they were grateful that nothing came of it. There was no sign of her. But as soon as Siss was allowed to get up she would have to go there, she was told.

The radiant image from the nights when she had had

fever : Unn, not lost, not dead, standing there as she had done that time in her own room.

Hallo, Siss.

Then Siss was up. Tomorrow she was to start school again, and dreaded it. Today she was to go to see Auntie, now left alone. There was no question of avoiding it. She set out from home.

A bright winter's day. Mother had asked somewhat cautiously whether she should go with her to see Auntie? Going there might be difficult in many respects. It looked as if Mother was uncertain about sending Siss.

' No, you mustn't,' said Siss hurriedly.

' Why not?'

' Nobody is to come with me.'

Then Father interfered. 'Mother had better go with you today, Siss. Don't you remember how it was when you were asked about one thing and another?'

Mother said : ' She'll have to ask you about Unn.'

' No.'

' She will. She'll ask about everything. Unn may have told you. She won't ask so much if someone else is with you.'

' Nobody is to come with me,' said Siss, afraid.

' All right, if you insist,' they said, and gave in. ' You must do as you wish.'

Siss knew that she should have let her mother go with her. Her parents were hurt. They did not know that she *had* to be alone with Auntie.

Siss walked quickly to the solitary house. The trees round it were bent with the weight of the snow. It looked empty, but the path leading to the doorstep was cleared. It must have been done by a man; Auntie could not have managed it so well. Somebody must be concerned about her, and coming to clear the path for her. Perhaps she was not alone after all? Siss walked in, full of dread.

Auntie was alone.

'Oh, it's you,' she said as soon as Siss opened the door. 'How nice of you to come. Are you well again? I heard you were ill after that trip to the river.'

'I'm all right again now. I'm to start school tomorrow.'

Suddenly she felt no dread. Instead it was safe and right to be sitting there.

Auntie continued: 'I knew that was why you didn't come, because you couldn't. It wasn't because you didn't dare, or because you thought it would be awkward. But I've been expecting you.'

Siss did not reply.

Auntie left her to sit for a little while. Then she came and sat down beside her.

'Perhaps you'd like to ask me about Unn?' she said. 'You must ask if you want to.'

'What?' said Siss, who had been sitting steeling herself for questions.

'What do you most want to ask?'

'Nothing,' said Siss.

'Is it *so* secret?' asked Auntie, and Siss did not understand her.

Then she exclaimed: 'Aren't they going to find her soon?'

'I hope they will every day, but . . .'

Didn't Auntie believe it any more? Her voice sounded a little strange.

' Would you like to look in?'

' Yes.'

Auntie opened the door of the little bedroom. Siss took a quick look to see if everything was the same as before. The mirror, the chair, the bed, the album on its shelf. That was there. Of course, not many days had passed since—

But nothing in here must be disturbed, she thought. It must stay like that till she comes back.

' Sit down in the chair,' said Auntie.

Siss sat in the chair, as she had done last time. Auntie sat on the edge of the bed, it was rather odd. Then Siss burst out : ' Why *is* Unn like this?'

' Isn't Unn as she should be, then?' asked Auntie cautiously.

They were careful to talk as if Unn were alive.

Siss replied defiantly : ' Unn's nice.'

' Yes, and wasn't she happy too, the other evening?'

' She wasn't *only* happy,' said Siss, forgetting.

' I didn't know Unn before she lost her mother last spring,' said Auntie. ' Of course I had met her, but I didn't know her. And you know her even less, Siss. She can't be only happy when her mother died so soon.'

' There was something else too.'

Siss started as she said it. Too late. It was dangerous to be in there.

' Oh?' said Auntie unconcernedly.

Siss retreated hastily. ' Oh, I don't *know* anything. She didn't tell me anything about it.'

There she was again—in the fateful circle from which she could not escape. Auntie came up to her. Siss was embarrassed and nervous. What Unn had said was for her, Siss, and not for her kind aunt.

Auntie stood over her and told her: 'They've been here asking and asking until I'm just about worn out, Siss. Asking about everything to do with Unn. I know they've been at you too. They had to, there was nothing else to do.'

She paused. Siss was nervous. She had known it would end like this if she came, but still . . . She must brace herself.

'You must forgive my asking you too, but I am Unn's aunt—and I think there is a difference. You see, I know nothing about Unn, except what everyone else knows and has seen. She didn't tell me anything, and that's how it was all the time. Did Unn say anything special to you that evening?'

'No!'

Auntie looked at her. Siss returned her gaze defiantly. Auntie retreated.

'No, of course you don't know any more than we do. It's not likely that Unn would have told you all sorts of things the very first time you met.'

'No, it isn't,' said Siss, determined not to be shaken now.

'But supposing Unn doesn't come back?' she asked without thinking, gave a start, and regretted it.

'You shouldn't ask that, Siss.'

'No.'

She got a reply to her questions all the same.

'You may as well know that I've thought about that too. If Unn doesn't come back, I shall sell this house and go away. I don't think I can stay here—even though I had Unn for only six months.

'Well, well,' she added. 'We won't talk about *that*. It doesn't mean that Unn won't come back just because she hasn't done so yet. Nothing shall be disturbed here, don't worry.'

How could she have known *that*? thought Siss.

' I must go home,' she said anxiously.

'Yes, of course you must. Thank you for coming.'

She thinks I know something. I shan't come again.

Auntie was just as placid and friendly as she had been the whole time.

Siss hurried home. A good thing that was over and done with.

8

School

Siss arrived in the schoolyard the next morning. As usual it was not quite daylight yet.

They surrounded her at once. Three or four of them who were there already stood round her in a circle. Siss was popular.

'Oh, there you are!'

'Are you better?'

'Was it awful that night?'

'And just think, they can't find a trace of Unn!'

Siss answered yes and no. They stared at her a little, but took it no further.

More came, and soon Siss was standing in a tight circle. Not just the girls, the boys as well. They were all about the same age. In all the rumpus they would willingly have done whatever Siss told them to. She saw the happiness in their eyes at this renewed morning meeting. It was good to see, but she did not for a moment forget her solemn promise. It was here that it would be tested.

'We went out searching too,' a few of them told her proudly.

'Yes, I know.'

What had happened to Unn had filled the days with tension and shock—with Unn at the centre like a dark shadow. It was already easier to think about; they were no longer part of it—and here was Siss standing among them looking almost the same as before. They were happy. She noticed one or two of them whom she had previously had to reckon with as equals, but who now stood there embarrassed and happy too. She could not help noticing it— and because she had made the promise and was going to keep away from them, she remembered scores of pleasant things they had done together. And because she had made the promise all this became a lump in her throat.

The atmosphere was tense. Not for the friendly crowd, but for Siss it was all of a sudden distinctly tense.

Somebody could not help asking a question that was in everyone's mind : ' What *was* it?'

Siss started as if cut with a knife, but it was too late to stop the questioner : ' They say Unn told you something you wouldn't—'

Someone said sharply : ' Hush !'

But too late. It was done. At that very moment when Siss had so little resistance it came pouring over her yet again. She found herself jumping at them. She was energetic and used to be able to jump so as to scare them, so she jumped at them shouting wildly : ' I can't stand it !'

Then she threw herself into the heap of snow right in front of them and burst into tears.

The circle stood at a loss. They had not expected this; it was so unlike the Siss they knew. Siss lay there crying. Finally one of the boys went over and dug down to her with his snow-covered boot. The others looked at each other or away. The weather was thick and blind again that day, and seemed to be saying boo !

The boy did not say it.

'Siss,' he said, very kindly, and nudged her with his boot.

She looked up at him.

That one?

He had always been in the background before; nobody had bothered about him, he just tagged along.

She got up, and nobody said anything. They brushed the snow off her back with quick strokes. And then fortunately the teacher arrived to begin the ordinary school day.

Siss was given a friendly nod from the charge desk when they were all in their places. She was certain he would not question her once.

'All right again, Siss?'

'Yes.'

'That's good.'

It was sufficient. At once the atmosphere was easier. She thought too about the boy who had nudged her so kindly with his boot. She could see the back of his neck from where she was sitting. She was grateful, the morning turned out to be easier than she had expected, much easier than it had looked with that unfortunate beginning. There seemed to be such a thin, thin cover on everything.

She had looked quickly to see whether Unn's place had been kept empty. Yes, nobody had moved there, even though it would have been convenient, the way the desks were placed.

Siss was left in peace for the rest of the day. She stood alone by the wall, and the others accepted this for the time being. They were probably rather ashamed after what had happened that morning. And there was no whispering or chatter about Unn and the search; they had probably whispered themselves out and become tired of it. It had only flamed up for a moment when Siss arrived. After all, Unn had never really been one of them; she had been an outsider, acquiring respect, but nothing more.

Siss suddenly noticed that she was standing by the wall just as Unn had done, while the noise of play rose up a short distance away, just as usual. One of the girls looked as if she had taken over the leadership in a short space of time.

And I'm going to stand here. I've promised.

The noise merely continued.

Siss did not reflect on the fact that it merely continued, but it was rather strange and unfamiliar to be standing as she was now. It felt like that to begin with, then it was a relief.

The days righted themselves and gathered speed. Christmas came as usual. Not as usual for Siss though, for she stayed at home and invited nobody. They allowed her to do as she liked; gradually everyone had realized how tense Siss was. Out of doors the snow piled higher.

The snow piled higher, and still Unn did not appear.

The search was probably going on somewhere or other —here in the drifts there was no longer any sign of it. People were probably not thinking about it every day either. The snow sifted down, blanketing everything, out of doors and in people's minds.

Auntie, all alone, did not visit anyone during the Christmas holiday, but there were people who visited her. Siss did not dare. She waited in fear for the news that Auntie had sold her house and was going to move. When she did that, she would have given up all hope.

Auntie was still there.

Siss had a desire to go to her mother and ask : 'Don't you think about Unn any more either?'

It looked as if everyone had forgotten Unn. Siss never heard her mentioned. She did not ask her mother, but she felt as if she were alone with a burden which would become too heavy. She thought often about the night at the ice palace; the men seemed to have made *that* the place. When the surface became right for ski-ing towards spring she would go there.

All the same she went to her mother and made her accusation, but in more general terms : 'They're not thinking about Unn any more.'

'Who isn't?'

'Nobody is !' said Siss, even though she had not meant to. It had gone dark, and then she had said it.

Her mother answered calmly : 'How do you know, my girl?'

Siss said nothing.

'And then nobody knew Unn. It's unreasonable, but it makes it seem different. People have a lot to think about, you see.' Mother looked at Siss and added : '*You're the person who can think about Unn all the time.*'

As if Siss had been given a great gift.

9

The Gift

Now it is night—and what is this?

It is the gift.

I don't understand.

It is night and I have been given a great gift.

Been given something and I don't know what it is. I don't understand at all. The gift looks at me wherever I go.

The gift stands and waits.

It isn't snowing now, it's clear weather. The drifts are huge. They have wiped out all the traces that might have been made, filled up all the hiding places. Great stars hang above the snow, and my gift stands outside and waits for me, or comes in and sits down with me.

I feel I have been given it, and yet . . .

It's not windy either. If a storm were to set in, the loose snow would start swirling. The wind would roar and moan in the hills—but my gift is indoors and is for me and waits for me.

It's quiet indoors; quiet up in the topmost attic with the dark little window. I believe my gift is standing up there at the window now, looking out—as it waits for me to see it.

It is everywhere I go, and I know that this is a great gift. What shall I do with it?

It was silly of me to have been frightened: there's nobody at the sides of the road. Unn will most likely come when the mild wind brings the thaw.

She'll come if the mild wind has to blow a thousand times! I know she will and I shan't think about anything else. I have been given a great gift.

10

The Bird

The wild bird with steel claws drew a slanting stripe between two peaks, in no time at all. He did not settle, but
climbed once more, slicing his way on. No rest, no certain
goal for his perpetual flight.

Beneath him spread the winter landscape. It was desolate where he travelled. He sliced it into shreds beneath
his eyes. His eyes seemed to send invisible lightning and
splinters of glass through the frosty air, and they saw
everything.

Here he was master—and it was empty of life for that
reason. His bristling claws were cold as ice. The freezing
wind moaned between them as he flew.

The bird, slicing up the desolate moors into shreds and
spirals, was death. If, after all, something was alive down
among the bushes or trees, the eye would flash lightning
and a slanting stripe slice down, leaving even less life than
before.

He saw nothing that resembled himself.

He hovered above the great moors daily, perpetually in
flight, never tired.

He will not die.

A violent snowstorm had passed over the moors. In ex-
posed places the snow had been blown away. The drifts

were loose, there had been no mild spell to pack them.
Now they were whirled into enormous waves. Clear weather
followed with cold sunshine. High above, in the air above
the ice palace, the slashing eye of the bird watched these
alterations of contour.

Today the snow on the palace had been swept away, so
that it appeared in its true shape. The bird noticed the
change and sent a lightning slash downwards: the splinter-
ing eyes first, and himself following. He made an abrupt
turn in the middle of his stripe, swung in order to brake,
came on again and sliced close by the wall of ice. Then
he climbed to a dizzy height and turned into a small black
speck in the sky.

The next moment he was on his way down again.
Another line was drawn in front of the ice palace, at precisely the same point. He was an unfettered bird, threatened
by no one, at liberty to do as he liked, to be fascinated
when he so wished.

He could not leave the spot. Nor could he pounce, or
settle—only slice past the ice wall like a dark puff of wind.
The next minute far away on the horizon, or spiralling
upwards; the next moment past the ice wall again at the
same point. He was no longer a completely unfettered bird
with steel claws and accompanying wind. He was bound
fast here, the prisoner of his own freedom, unable to give
up. What he saw confused him.

He would cut himself fatally with his own shreds—as
hard as glass where they showed the least. But they ripped
up the air; he could not avoid being ripped up himself.

II

An Empty Seat

School and the winter took their usual course. Siss stood by the wall in the breaks. The others had become used to it. The weeks passed, each one like the next. The big search for Unn had been shelved.

Siss stood by the wall, keeping her promise. A new girl had taken over as leader of the group.

On such a winter's morning a strange girl entered the classroom. She was the same age as the others, and had come to join their class. Her parents had moved to the district a couple of days ago.

At once the atmosphere was tense. Siss saw, with a start of surprise, that they had not forgotten. The empty desk left by Unn was immediately the centre of attention. The girl stood there, a stranger to it all, looking about her. The others went to their places.

The girl saw there was a vacant place in the middle of the room, and took a couple of steps towards it. Then she paused, and asked them, ' Is this one free?'

They all looked at Siss : Siss who of late had become a different person; Siss whom they longed to get back again. Now they could show her how interested they were in her. Siss felt their sympathy like a wave, and it rebounded back from her, while her cheeks coloured : a fleeting joy she had not imagined possible.

'No,' she said to the girl, out of all these sensations.

The girl looked surprised.

'It's *never* free,' said Siss, and the whole class straightened up in their desks in a common recognition of something they had not known they felt: that they suddenly wished to defend Unn's place. They looked at the innocent newcomer with dislike, as if she had already disgraced herself.

There were no more desks, and the girl remained standing in front of the class until the teacher arrived. The tension increased.

'And now let's find you a desk,' he said, when the introductions were over. He looked at the class for a moment before taking the obvious decision. 'You'd better take that desk there. It's free now.'

The girl looked across at Siss.

Siss stood up. 'It's n-not free,' she stuttered.

The teacher met her eyes and said calmly: 'The desk ought to be used, Siss. I think that would be the best way.'

'No!'

The teacher was in a quandary. He looked at the class and sensed from their expressions that they agreed with Siss.

'There are desks out in the corridor that aren't being used,' said Siss, still on her feet.

'Yes, I know there are.'

He turned to the newcomer. 'The desk belonged to a girl who disappeared last autumn. I expect you read about it in the papers.'

'Lots of times.'

'And if her place isn't there, she'll never come back!' exclaimed Siss—and at that moment her wild assertion did not seem absurd. A quiver passed through them all.

The teacher said, 'I think that's going too far, Siss. None of us should say things like that.'

'But can't the desk stay as it is?'

'I like the way you feel, Siss, but you mustn't go too far. Wouldn't it be better for someone to sit there for the time being? That would be quite natural. Nothing would be spoilt by that, would it?'

'Yes, it would,' said Siss, unable to think very far ahead in the tumult of the moment. She stared, shocked at the teacher, who could not understand her either.

The new girl was still standing in front of the class, unable to join them. It was obvious that she would have preferred to run away from it all. There was clearly a feeling of ill-will against her for which she was not responsible. The class sat securely behind Siss in a topsy-turvy kind of satisfaction.

The teacher came to a decision.

'All right, I'll fetch another desk.'

Siss looked at him gratefully.

'It's not worth spoiling a thing like this,' he added. He went out into the corridor.

At once their attitude towards the girl was changed. She was no enemy, she was welcome.

For some reason they asked Siss, who was crouching in her seat again : 'You'll join us again now, won't you, Siss?'

She shook her head.

She could not tell them about the promise and that she had been given a great gift. All she was waiting for at that moment was to turn towards the teacher who came dragging the desk.

12

A Dream of Snow-Covered Bridges

As we stand the snow falls thicker.
Your sleeve turns white.
My sleeve turns white.
They move between us like
snow-covered bridges.

But snow-covered bridges are frozen.
In here is living warmth.
Your arm is warm beneath the snow, and
a welcome weight on mine.

It snows and snows
upon silent bridges.
Bridges unknown to all.

13

Black Creatures on the Snow

A movement up in the tree-tops is the first warning.
There is no wind, merely a current through the green tops
of the conifers in the early evening. Only when night falls
will it become a strong draught, a nocturnal stream.

Snow has fallen today too. Everything is shining new and
white, but the sky is heavy, the clouds low and smooth.

Now it begins. People out walking in it feel it and change
to a different rhythm, as if wanting to get home in good
time. How mild it is, they say to themselves. But they have
no desire to speak. Now it begins.

The stream has increased, and is flowing more strongly up
in the forest. The pine needles stretch their tongues and sing
an unfamiliar nocturnal song. Each tongue is so small that
it cannot be heard; together the sound is so deep and
powerful that it could level the hills if it wished. But the
air is mild, the snow lies wet and unmoving below, no
longer rising in snow flurries.

How mild it is, say the people out walking late. They
leave the forest and come out on to open ground—and
there they meet the mild stream itself. They are moved,
and welcome it as they would a friendly envoy. It has been
cold long enough—and it will probably be just as bitter
again soon. But in this wind they are for a moment as

they prefer to be. The wet wind in the winter darkness can make the face radiant.

Nothing has yet been released, but something will come; it is tied by its own warning up in the clouds. In this state they finally return from their walk to the sleeping house. No one will know tomorrow that for a little while this evening they were radiant and altered.

In the morning and when it gets light it is still very mild, with the trees soughing and swaying. When the daylight comes the wet snow is seen to be scattered with minute black creatures; on every inch of snow, and for miles in all directions. They are alive, creeping as if on the move; recently they were a cloud, windborne and nightborne, a glimpse of what goes on in the universe, and they will turn into a stripe in the drift after the next snowfall.

14

The Vision in March

March arrived with its clear sky after all the mid-winter weather. Now the mornings came early, shining and frosty. The drifts had settled, making for good ski-ing. It was the time for ski trips, the time for the trip to the ice palace. It was the end of March now.

The class had decided on the ski trip one Saturday just before they went home. They would go on Sunday morning. The trip would be extra special, because Siss was coming with them.

They decided they had won Siss over. Three of them had approached her.

'Come with us on the trip, Siss. Just this once.'

They were the three she liked best.

'Oh no,' she said.

Just those three. The group knew who to send.

The three had no intention of giving in at the first refusal.

'Come with us, Siss. You simply can't go on cutting us like this. We haven't done anything to you.'

Siss had a strong current against her. She intended to go to the ice palace on her own, and yet . . .

The one of the three who knew she was the strongest took a step forward and said softly, 'Siss, we want you to come with us.'

'Siss,' she repeated, even more softly, making it into a dangerous weapon of temptation. The other two stood stock-still, giving even more effect to her words.

And they were too strong. The promise was pushed a little aside. Siss answered in the same dangerous tone as her tempter had used and with which one answers tempters : 'All right, I'll come. But if I come we're going to the ice palace.'

The three of them glowed : 'Now you're being sensible.'

Siss had a guilty conscience as soon as she was alone. But Father and Mother were so happy when they heard about it that the hurt seemed to come from that source.

In the morning the group collected and set out with a lot of shouting and noise. It was a frosty, clear morning, with a little loose snow on top of the firm foundation, as it should be when at its best. Everyone was pleased that the trip would take them past the waterfall, and there was general rejoicing that Siss was with them. Siss was conscious of their friendliness; it sustained her buoyantly as her skis did on the snow-crust with the new snow on top.

Everything was and was not as it should be.

They followed a track that would bring them to the river just below the waterfall. Here were great silent pools where ice had formed and where you could cross over if you wished. The waterfall roared in the silence; they went right up to it.

All of them had been here to see the ice palace once or twice during the winter, so it did not take their breath away —yet it towered above them, powerful and mysterious. It was shining and free of snow now. The March sun had found the way to it early today, and was playing over the ice formations.

They conscientiously remembered to say nothing to Siss about dangerous subjects. She understood this, and felt simultaneously secure and embarrassed. She was secretly in tumult at the sight of this place again. The men had cemented the link between the palace and herself that night; she would have to stay behind, and take leave of the others here.

They feasted their eyes on the palace, listened to the roar of the falls which would soon become much stronger —and then they were ready to go on.

Siss stood stock-still. What they feared had happened. It had occurred to them that perhaps they had not won her over after all. They stood waiting for her to say so.

'Look,' she said, 'I don't think I'll go any further. I really only wanted to come here.'

'Why?' asked someone. But one of the three tempters said at once : 'Siss must decide. If she doesn't want to come any further it's none of our business.'

'No. I'll turn back here,' said Siss, with her usual expression when she wanted to prevent opposition.

'We'll turn back too, then,' they said generously.

Siss was embarrassed. 'No, of course not. Please. Can't you go on as you've planned? I'd like to be here alone for a bit.'

Their faces fell. Can't we stay with you? was written on them plainly. The solemn way she had talked about being there alone reminded them of how Siss had been all winter. It made them silent and constrained.

Siss saw from their expressions that the day was spoilt, but as far as she was concerned there was nothing to be done. It was too late, the promise had risen up inside her like a wall.

'So you don't want to be with us any more today?'

'No, I'd rather not. You don't understand, I know. It's something I've promised,' she said, startling them.

When she said it like that, they dimly realized that it was a promise made to Unn, and nobody knew whether she was alive or dead. In that case it was powerful and dangerous. It put a stop to all discussion.

'You know I can find my way home on my own. I have our tracks to follow.'

Since she spoke so normally they regained their voices and were able to reply, and even argue.

'Yes, of course,' they said, 'but it's not that.'

'You've been standing by the wall the whole winter,' one of them dared to say.

'And we thought everything was going to be as it used to be.'

'I'll get home before you do,' said Siss, who had no desire to discuss the matter.

'Yes, but we thought everything *was* as it used to be, you see.'

'Go on, and don't talk like that,' she pleaded.

They nodded to her and then, one by one, began to ski down the slope. They collected again on a small plateau, stood there as if in conference, and then swung away in a tightly-knit group.

Siss, shamefaced and unhappy, ran on her floating skis back to the waterfall and the walls of ice. The roar drew her as if a voice were calling.

The memory of the men. They had stood here so strangely that night, as if something unexpected was about to happen. Because they believed it might have happened here. There was nowhere else to go when at one's wits' end.

She repeated the thought : I am at my wits' end. The sort of thing people said many times a day without meaning it.

Shamefaced and unhappy she ran away from her companions and straight into the roar, straight towards the ice palace.

It was just as alarmingly tall and strange from whichever angle you looked at it. Polished and sparkling, free of snow, and with a ring of cold around it in the middle of the mild March air in which it stood. The river, black and deep, moved out from under the ice, gathering speed on its way downward and taking with it everything that could be torn away.

Siss stood there for a long time. She wished she could have stood as the men had done before they left, just before the start of the sombre song. *They* had stood in the flickering lantern-light as if they expected the missing child to emerge before their very eyes and tell them that there was nothing to find. Siss could not believe such a thing.

A great bird sliced past, making her start, but by that time it was already out of sight.

Nothing to search for here, nothing to find. But all the same . . . For the sake of the grown men . . .

She decided to stay. She took off her skis and walked on the firm snow up along the ice wall. The ice palace alone was fascinating enough, the way it had built itself up out of spurting and trickling moisture. Now all of it was compact and strong. Siss decided to go to the very top, to climb about there, simply to be there.

When she came up she looked out over a confusion of ice shapes. It was all blown clean of snow. Cautiously she let herself slide out on to the sloping ice, down into deep gulleys, half afraid that it might not be strong enough after all—and with the gnawing thought: perhaps it was like *this*, exactly like this that it happened?

Just now she had left her friends shamefacedly. Now she was shamefaced because she had somehow betrayed something when she went with them, forgotten her promise for the tempting eyes and lips of friendship, and a ski trip. No, not the ski trip, but it had meant a great deal to be with them, it had gradually become more difficult to resist. She had resisted until she was worn out.

Siss's feelings were in tumult up there on the tall, intricate dome of ice. She let herself slide along gulleys and down into fissures and came out on to a shelf some way down and at the very edge, facing the sun and the falls. She was in tumult on account of the place. She climbed down a hollow of transparent, solid ice. The sun shone on it and sparkled in hundreds of different patterns.

She screamed as she did so: for there was Unn! Straight in front of her, looking out through the ice wall.

In a flash she thought she saw Unn, deep in the ice.

The strong March sun was shining directly on her, so that she was wreathed in glinting brightness, all kinds of shining streaks and beams, curious roses, ice roses and ice ornaments, decked as if for some great festivity.

Siss, paralysed from head to foot, took it all in. For a moment she was unable to move or to make a sound beyond her first scream. She realized she was seeing a vision. She often heard about people who had had visions; now she was one of them. She was seeing a vision, seeing Unn, for the brief while she could bear to look at all.

The vision did not fade, it seemed. It remained unmoving in the ice—but it was too overpowering for Siss to look at. It had come like an assault.

Unn was enormous in this vision behind the running ice walls, much bigger than she should have been. It was really only her face that showed; the rest of her was vague.

Sharp rays of light cut across the picture, coming from unseen fissures and angles. There was a dazzling brilliance about Unn that made it difficult to grasp. Siss could not bear the sight. She regained the use of her limbs and crawled over into other hollows, without a thought other than that of hiding. She had gazed too long as it was; she was trembling.

When she came to her senses she was a good distance away. She thought: it must have disappeared by now, too. Visions do disappear quickly.

So it must have meant that Unn was dead.

Of course. Unn is dead.

Siss went to pieces as the realization struck her. This thing that she had not wanted to think, had not mentioned to herself, but which had been a horror in the background all the time—and which people round about had certainly said so often and so openly—now there was no way of avoiding it. She had to believe it.

As she lay thinking she heard a swish close behind her, felt a sudden puff of wind, saw a streak in the air—all at once. Very close.

She shivered. It was cold lying on the ice. She began to crawl along in the slippery cavities. The way back was more difficult. Beneath her, in the ice, there was a curious play of sparkling fissures and light effects all the time. Occasionally it looked dangerous; she slid on to places without intending to. But she managed to climb up again.

When she reached the top everything seemed so depressing and difficult. She stood looking out and began to wonder whether she really had seen anything.

Of course she had.

And she thought: One day in the spring this whole mountain of ice will be smashed to smithereens. It will crack up, and the flood-water will take it, smash it, tear it away on its downward course, dash it into even smaller fragments against the rocks, and wash it all out into the lower lake—and that will be the end of it.

Siss imagined herself standing there that day, watching it happen. She imagined too for a second that she was standing up on the ice palace at that moment—but she rejected the thought immediately.

No.

Siss found her skis again. Instead of putting them on she sat down on the warm wood on the warm, sunny slope. She had not yet come to her senses sufficiently. She was bewildered by the vision of Unn, ornamented with ice.

One thing was certain: she could never tell anyone about this. Not anyone in the whole world!

Why should she have seen this? Had she forgotten Unn too often?

Not a word to Father and Mother; not a word to Auntie, not to anyone.

Had she seen it? Had she perhaps dozed off up there in the sun, and dreamed for an instant? When she looked about her in the sunshine, sitting on her skis, it was easy to believe she had imagined it all.

No, it wasn't so easy as that. She was quivering all over. That doesn't happen after a brief dream.

She managed to put on her skis with trembling fingers. She looked up at the ice palace and thought : I expect I'm seeing it for the last time. I daren't come here again.

And she set her skis in motion.

Siss came home tired and sweating after her run. They saw, crestfallen, that all was not as it should be.

'Are you back already? Did you feel ill?'

'No, it's nothing.'

'But we know the others won't be coming home for a long time yet. We phoned to find out.'

'I turned back at the waterfall.'

'But why?'

'It's nothing,' she replied to their nervous questions. 'I felt I couldn't manage the whole trip, and so I went with them as far as the river.'

'*You* couldn't manage it?'

'I'm all right now, though. I felt I couldn't manage it just for a while.'

Her explanation did not ring true. She was not usually the first to give up.

'We're upset about this,' said her father.

'Yes. We were happy today. We thought you'd got over it at last,' said her mother. 'We thought things were going to be just as they used to be.'

Got over it, they said.

They cut right through and drew out the truth about what she was expected to do : get over it. It was easy to say, but how could that happen as long as the vision was dancing before her eyes? She realized she had lied to little purpose; they could not be taken in. But at any rate she could keep her mouth shut. She would willingly have pleased them in some way at that moment, but could not lie to do so—and how else could she do so? She looked at her mother in silence.

'Go and take a bath and wash off all that sweat,' said Mother. 'Then we can talk about it later.'

'What should we talk about later?'

'Off you go. The water's hot.'

Her mother's usual advice when she came home after some tussle or other: into the bath tub. Go and take a bath.

She lay in the warm water, but saw the face among flashing ice roses and glinting light. It was ever-present. The fatigue and well-being after such a trip were waiting over in the corner, but were unable to approach. Here were walls of ice with a face inside them four times too big.

Something enormous that she had to bear alone, that had to be hidden among her innermost thoughts, among the thoughts she never dared let pass her lips.

It said: Siss.

No no, it said nothing.

But the face was just behind the warm steam.

Siss? it said. Panic lay in wait, in spite of the bath. It had lain in wait all the way home, now it seized her. There were ice walls, eyes—

'Mother!' she shouted.

Mother was there in a trice as if she had been expecting it. Siss was small. But she did not forget to keep silent about what had happened.

15

A Test

What about the promise now?

What is this that is about me? A nudging wind, playing affectionately with my hair. A gentle wind—as if unpractised.

Unn will never come back to meet me, as the promise said. What of it, then, now that Unn is dead?

Siss stood by herself again at school the next day, and went home alone. She had to shut herself in when she got there. The vision in the ice palace had been so powerful that she had to guard against talking about it all the time and wherever she might be. If she let it loose in front of others the panic would seize her.

She was forced to stay in her bedroom and read, or wander about alone out of doors. It was too dangerous to have her parents' eyes on her: they might breach the dam; it might spill over. They were expecting something, she knew very well. But she could not approach them. They could remark quite calmly: 'We see scarcely anything of you, Siss.'

'No,' she replied.

They said no more, although they had her cornered. It made her feel insecure.

Why did I see Unn?

So that I should not forget her?

Of course.

It seemed to her that Unn was forgotten. Nobody talked about her; she never heard the name mentioned. Not at home, not at school. As if Unn had never existed, thought Siss, outraged.

I'm the only one who remembers. And her Auntie, I expect she remembers. And she hasn't sold her house and gone away.

Who else thinks about Unn?

The question was urgent. It was so important that Siss had to test it. She tested it one morning in the classroom just before a lesson. Everybody was there except the teacher. She did not want him mixed up in this. She had to brace herself to do it.

She made her stand, plucked up courage, and spoke at the room so that everyone could hear, making it sound almost like an announcement: ' *Unn.*'

Just the bare name. She could do it in no other way. They would probably understand.

Nothing happened immediately, if that was what she had expected. Their faces turned towards her, of course, and the chatter ceased, but after that there was merely a silence.

They were probably waiting for further surprises. When nothing came they began to exchange glances. Still nobody uttered a sound. Siss thought they seemed shocked. She looked round her cautiously.

Was there a wall of animosity? No, there was no wall. They were perplexed.

She was perplexed too. She should never have thought of it.

At last someone replied. It was not one of the girls and therefore close to her, but the boy who had nudged her with his boot. She had noticed that he had come to the fore on various occasions recently. It was he who replied sharply : 'We haven't forgotten her.'

As if cutting off something.

One of the girls joined in. 'No, of course we haven't—if that's what you think.'

Siss was burning with shame. She realized that she was on the wrong track in her isolation. She stammered, 'No, it was only—'

She ducked down, nonplussed on account of all she could have told them and that would have caused them distress.

Part Three

WOODWIND PLAYERS

I

Auntie

I'm not alone in remembering, but this is something people aren't talking about. Why don't they talk about it? It's unlike them.

Siss started occasionally at the thought: Now the cottage is sold, Auntie's cottage. Now Auntie will go.

The next day she went past it on her way home. She saw that someone was still there, and that Auntie's things were outside.

Since the house isn't sold, Auntie believes it.

Siss was caught one day as she was passing the house in this way. She had come too near and was seen. Auntie came to the door and beckoned to her.

'Come here, Siss!'

When she came, reluctant and tense, Auntie said, 'I believe I promised to tell you if I were to sell and leave.'

'Yes. Have you?'

Auntie nodded.

So it was sold. What has she found out? At the same moment as I was at the ice palace? Nonsense. Say more, wished Siss, and Auntie did so. She said without evasion: 'I'm certain now that there's nothing more to wait for.'

'Do you *know* that?'

135

'I don't *know*, and yet—I do know just the same. So I've sold the cottage. And I'm going away.'

Strangely enough Siss felt secure. Auntie would not say: Now that I'm going, surely you can tell me everything that you didn't want to talk about before? She would not say it.

'Are you leaving tomorrow then?'

'Why do you say that? Why tomorrow?' Auntie looked at her sharply. 'Had you heard already?'

'No. But every day I've thought, I expect she'll leave tomorrow.'

'Well, you've guessed right at last, for I *am* leaving tomorrow. That was why I called to you; it was lucky I saw you going past. If you hadn't come by, I had thought of looking in on *you* this evening.'

Siss said nothing. It was strange to hear Auntie telling her that she was leaving. It was terribly sad. Auntie was silent for a while too, but then she remembered something.

'Besides, I called you because I'd like to go for a walk this evening just the same. My last evening. I wanted to ask whether you'd come with me?'

A twinge of joy.

'Yes! Where do you want to go?'

'Nowhere. I just want to walk about for a bit.'

'But I must go home first. I came straight from school.'

'Oh, there's plenty of time. I shan't go until it gets quite dark. And the twilight doesn't come so early any more.'

'I'll go at once.'

'You must say we'll be late,' said Auntie, 'but there's no need to be nervous.'

Siss felt quite solemn as she walked home. She and

Auntie were going for a walk. It would be no ordinary walk.

'We shall be late,' said Siss at home when she was ready to go. 'She said I was to tell you.'

'Yes, that's all right,' they both answered with alacrity.

Siss knew perfectly well why they were so agreeable. Anything she could find to do was welcomed at this time, even if it was no more than an evening walk with someone else. She had brought them to this pass.

She thought about it all the way back to Auntie.

Auntie was not ready.

'There's no haste,' she said. 'We shan't go before it gets dark. We want to be on our own; this isn't anyone else's business.'

Siss was happy and excited, and it was all mixed up with the sadness of departure. Auntie was busy packing and tidying things. Siss helped her as far as she could—but most of it was already finished. The sitting-room was stripped and bare, cheerless, and much larger than before.

The door to the bedroom had not been left open. That was a good thing.

'I expect you'd like to look in?'

'No.'

'No, there's no point. There's not a scrap left.'

'I'm sorry, I think I will after all.'

She looked in. There was not a scrap left. Such things are odd, and make you feel insecure.

Now they could go; it was getting dark.

The spring was clearly on its way. You felt it when you stepped out of a house: the soft air, and the snow that had a spring smell about it. But the snow still lay compactly everywhere. The sky was hung with low-lying cloud, the evening mild and dark. You could walk as slowly as you liked in that kind of weather. It was just as it should be, and they walked along slowly for a good while, without exchanging a word.

The landscape around them was indistinct. Indistinctly the houses stood aside for them. Lights shone out. Siss made no sound. Auntie was taking her farewell walk. Tomorrow she would not be here.

She'll probably say something shortly.

The winter-spring evening transformed the landscape into a hazy, shifting pattern that passed their eyes in slow movement, a wall slowly-pacing beside them. The shimmer of the snow made walking easy. Across the imperfect screen of their eyes there glided tall trees that seemed to stretch out their arms in admonition; and pitch-black, stooping-shouldered rocks, moving like clenched fists towards their foreheads.

This was Auntie's farewell. She was not visiting anybody; she had not had very much to do with other people while she lived here. She had been a friendly stranger who bothered no one and who preferred to manage on her own. But when misfortune had struck and the child was lost, everyone had volunteered their help. Now Siss watched while Auntie said good-bye in her own way.

So they walked in silence for a long time. But it was not only a farewell. Siss was waiting—and the moment came. Auntie stopped on the road and said in a tone of voice that was almost embarrassed: ' Siss, I didn't ask you to come *just* to have company.'

138

Siss answered quietly, ' I didn't think you had.'

' What is this to be, then? How I wish it were over. No, I don't really, but still . . .'

Auntie began walking along the snow-hushed road, in the raw air. Her voice was raw too when she spoke again.

' I may live alone, but people tell me one thing and another. I meet them here and there,' said Auntie. ' And I know you've had a hard and difficult winter.'

She stopped, as if to give Siss time.

I shan't—thought Siss, preparing to be on the defensive.

' I've heard that you've cut yourself off from your school friends, and even from your parents to a certain extent.'

Siss said quickly : ' I made a promise.'

' Yes, I realized it must have been something of the sort —and I suppose I ought to be grateful to you, for the sake of kinship, so to speak. I don't want you to tell me any more about it. But you mustn't promise so much that you destroy yourself, especially when there's no point in it any more.'

Siss said nothing and tried to understand what Auntie was driving at. She was not listening unwillingly.

' You've been ill,' said Auntie.

' They went on so until I couldn't stand it any more! About something I couldn't tell them. Over and over again—'

' Yes, yes, I know. You must remember it was at the very beginning when everything had to be tried in order to find some trace. I was in such straits that I tried as well, you know. We none of us realized that it was too hard on you.'

' They've stopped now.'

139

'Yes, they put a stop to it in the end, when things began to go wrong.'

Siss stared at Auntie's vague outline. 'Put a stop to it?'

'Yes. You say they've stopped. I don't suppose you've heard anyone mention the disaster for a long time now. To you, I mean. The doctor who came to see you put a stop to it. They've had it rubbed into them at school too.'

This was a complete surprise to Siss. She scarcely managed to say, '*What?*'

It was a good thing they could not see each other's faces clearly, she thought. Then they could not have talked about it. Auntie had chosen the right time for telling her.

'They took a serious view of it, as you know. You were very depressed. It's best for me to tell you, since I'm going away. I think you ought to know.'

Siss still stood silent. Here was the explanation of much that had surprised her. Auntie added : 'You can be told about it now, now that it's over. Now that we're not waiting any more.'

Siss exclaimed : 'Is it over? What's over?'

'Yes, I thought we'd better talk about that too.'

Siss's heart began to thud, but Auntie began talking again, about the same thing.

'You mustn't think people have forgotten who they were searching for. They haven't forgotten, *I* know that. They've given me so much help that now I'm leaving I don't know what to do about it. I ought to have gone round to thank them all. But I can't, I'm not made that way.'

'No ...'

'And that's why I'm walking out here in the dark this evening. I'm too miserable. I want to walk about here, and yet I daren't show my face.'

And she did look miserable, standing there in the darkening April evening; but she didn't seem like it, really.

'Let's walk on, Siss. I'd like to do the rounds before I go to bed.'

The road again led among houses and people. The windows were still lighted here and there. Siss thought how good it was to be out walking with Auntie. She asked herself why she never went walking like this with her mother? She could find no answer. Even though she was enormously fond of her, she was shy with her too. She could not think of any way she wanted her to be different, but she was shy. She was shy with her father too—even though she was specially good friends with him. What in the world was it that made this miserable little Auntie into someone she would walk with all night if necessary?

Yes, Siss could ask her.

'You must tell me what's over, the way you said.'

'It's over for *you.*'

'Oh no!'

'I think it is, you know. There's nothing for us to wait for. She's gone and she's not alive.'

A good thing it was dark.

A whisper from Siss: 'Have you found out somehow?'

'Not what *you* call finding out, and yet—I know just the same.'

Siss knew this was an important moment. Auntie cleared her throat and steeled herself to say something decisive.

'Listen, Siss, what I want to ask you before I leave is that you should try to go back to all that you used to have. You said you had made a promise. But it can't come to anything, when the other party to it isn't here any more. You can't bind yourself to her memory, and shut yourself away from what is natural for you. You would only be a bother to yourself and to others, and no one will thank you for it, far from it. You're already making your parents unhappy. Are you listening to this speech of mine?'

'Yes, yes!'

'Then listen: she will not come back, and you are freed from your promise.'

A fresh twinge.

'Freed from my promise?'

'Yes.'

'Can you do that?'

'Yes, I think I can, here and now.'

Auntie's voice had acquired a ring of authority. Siss did not know what to think. An avalanche of relief, and at the same time doubt.

Auntie gripped her arm: 'Shall we say that it is so? Make an agreement?'

'How can I know if it's true?' said Siss.

'If it's true?' asked Auntie, hurt.

'Yes, whether *you* can do it for me. Because it was I—'

'Has it gone so deep, Siss? But what I just said—you must have thought the same, now and again this spring?'

'Yes, I have, but . . .'

'It will be all right. So I can be a *little* happier about going away.'

'You are funny,' exclaimed Siss, gratefully.

This was something she did not dare acknowledge. Freed from it? Was she? Was it good or sad to be freed from it? You are funny, was all she could say.

'We must get a move on,' said Auntie. 'We mustn't be too late about coming home either.'

'No, but let's go as far as you want.'

142

Beside them glided the increasingly confused pattern of trees, houses and rocks; and occasionally soot-black patches. When the latter came gliding into sight, it went straight to the heart—what's *that*!—in this unbearable moment; but it was imagination each time, and her heart started up again, full of the coursing blood. It's we who are walking; the pattern doesn't move.

Auntie's voice: 'I say again, you must feel you are freed. It's not right for you to go on as you are. It's not like you. You're a different person.'

Don't answer. It's not meant to be answered. But it's like the gleaming of stars in a well. And no explanation.

They had finished their walk. It was black night. Auntie had gone the rounds. They came to Siss's house first. A single lamp shone, waiting for her; there was no sound.

'Well, here we are, and I'd like to say—' began Auntie, but Siss said quickly, 'No. I'll see you home.'

'Oh no, don't bother.'

'I'm not afraid of the dark.'

'I'm sure you're not, but . . .'

'May I?'

'Yes, of course you may.'

They set off once more. The sleeping house with the waiting lamp wheeled away. The road was deserted. They began to feel a little tired.

'It's not cold.'

'Not a bit,' said Auntie.

Siss ventured to ask: 'What will you do in the place where you're going to live?'

She did not know where it was; it had not been mentioned. Auntie was used to seeing to everything on her own.

'Oh, I shall have to busy myself with something or other. I'll find something,' she said. 'I've sold the house too, you know. Don't worry about me for an instant, Siss.'

'No.'

'I'm a worthless creature,' said Auntie shortly afterwards, when they were nearing her house, nearing the end of the evening. She began again : 'Worthless. The people here have done everything for me during this misfortune, and now I'm going like this when I ought to take my leave properly.

'What do you think, Siss?' she asked, when Siss made no reply.

'I don't know what to say.'

'And so I've been thinking that since you've been with me this evening, they'll get to know that I went the rounds, and that I did it as a way of thanking them. There's that too. I've counted on your telling them about it, and I'd be grateful if you would—though I know that only a worthless creature would think things out like that.'

Now they would have to say good-bye.

They were floating, almost at one with the darkness, reflecting no light. Their footsteps could not be heard. But their breathing could, and perhaps the heart. They mingled with other almost inaudible nocturnal stirrings, like a small vibration in long wires.

Afraid of the dark? No. Bright woodwind players had appeared and were walking along the sides of the road.

2

Like the Water Drop and the Twig

Who is freed?

No one, and yet . . .

No wild leap back to the others : Here I am! No one is freed, and yet it is as if woodwind players have arrived.

Like the water drop and the twig in the daytime. The naked, wet twig, the sodden snow caving in below, and the clear water drop down in the snow. The snow drift trickles away—and it has a black stripe inside it, a stripe of black creatures that undulates with the layer of snow over hill and dale and trickles away. A strange memory : a hurrying of black creatures in the darkness, league upon league in a mild night between the cold spells. Now everything is trickling away as yellow water or standing still in yellow puddles.

' Hi, Siss !'

A distant shout. A call from the other world.

You feel like the water drop and the twig. You are uncertain. You are anything but dead.

The promise has been lifted off, but you are not freed because of that. There is an unmoving weight all the same. You know too little.

Things happened as quick as flame.

Mother, revived : ' Siss, can you run an errand for me after school today?'

'Yes, of course.'

Why is it different now? What have they seen? Perhaps it is only myself that thinks so.

She walked along the road on her errand. Everything about her was bare. Drizzle, wind and swaying trees. What was it like at school today? Don't know, I don't pay much attention to anything. It would be no good running over to them. The promise was a strong tie, hard, but I knew where I stood. If it's gone, I don't know where I am. When there's a strange scent in the spring twilight, I know least of all.

Someone was coming, joining the road from the northern slope in the wind and rain. A half-grown boy from the neighbourhood; she knew him. The sweat was steaming off him; he was dressed for the rain, and warm. Something smoothed itself out inside her, something that had knotted itself against the headlong approach behind her back.

'Is that you, Siss?' he said, and she thought he brightened. 'I must say I'm glad to get on to the main road at last. 'I've been wading up that slope and the drifts there are knee deep. It's like walking in wet sand up to your knees.'

Siss smiled at him.

'Have you been far?'

'I'll say! But everywhere else is free of snow. I've been to the river,' he said.

'Did you go right to the river?'

'Yes, the ice is breaking up now.'

So she knew for certain: someone was still searching. She loved him from top to toe. She asked: 'Is the big piece of ice still standing?'

'Yes,' said the boy curtly, as if he had stopped short in

the middle of something and did not wish to go further. Siss did.

'Does it look just the same?'

'Yes, just the same.'

'It won't stand there much longer, will it?'

'Oh no, the river's very high and I expect it'll rise even higher.'

She was full of affection for him, on account of the exhausting walk. She must have shown it. A curious prickling.

'You can hear the roar from far away,' he explained gratuitously, dropping the curt tone he had used as soon as Siss began asking questions. 'And you can see the ice from a great distance.'

'Can you?' she said.

'Yes, from a hill quite close to here—if you want to see it too.'

'No, I don't want to.'

There was a pause. They were well aware that they were talking about the missing girl.

'I say, Siss,' he said abruptly, in a friendly tone of voice. What is it now? she thought.

'I've thought of saying something to you, if I happened to run into you,' he began, but was hesitant about going on, and it came out uncertainly : 'There's nothing more to be done about it, Siss.'

So he managed to say it. It was plain speaking. Siss did not reply.

'You must think about that now,' he said.

Yes, it was plain speaking, right enough. Right into the tenseness and exhaustion—but the strange thing was that the effect was different from before, there was no defiance or revolt. On the contrary, it was good to hear it.

She almost whispered: 'I don't see how you can know either.'

'You must excuse me,' he said.

'You with the dimples,' he added.

Her face was tilted upwards and wet with the drizzle. Raindrops trickled down her cheeks and wandered into her dimples. She looked away quickly. Best not to show how red she was. How glad she was.

'Bye,' he said. 'I must go home and change.'

'Bye,' said Siss.

He was going in the opposite direction, so she did not have to accompany him. He had his own circle somewhere far away from hers. He was a big fellow, almost grown-up.

Just because he had said that about her dimples. Could it make such a difference?

Oh yes. She knew that it did really.

And so there was still someone walking along the river, searching, coming home again tired. Walking there alone. After Auntie had left and everything. A search that was almost meaningless.

It had been a time of snow and a time of death and of closed bedrooms—and she had arrived bang on the other side of it, her eyes dimming for joy because a boy had said, 'You with the dimples.'

Woodwind players are walking at the sides of the road. You walk as fast as you can, and wish at the same time that the road would never end.

The road did come to an end, and she got home too soon: it was still obvious that something had happened.

' Is it fine out of doors?' asked her mother.
' Fine? It's windy and raining.'
' It can be fine all the same, can't it?'
Siss looked at her mother furtively. She never questioned
her more than was necessary.

Nor did she.

3

The Palace Closes

Ice-cold lightning flashes emerge from all the rents in the palace, out into the desolate landscape and out into space. The course of the day alters their form and direction, but still the whole palace flashes from within and *out* towards the sun. The bird whose flight is bound fast to the place still makes slashes of steel right across it. He comes no nearer than he did the first time.

The ice palace is not searching for anything, it merely sends out light from its disintegrating chambers. This is a spectacle observed by no one. People do not pass this way.

The palace sends out flashes of lightning, and the bird has not yet slashed himself to death.

A spectacle observed by no one.

It will not last much longer now. The palace will fall. What the bird will do, nobody knows. The bird will rise like a speck into the sky, wild with fear, when the palace is shattered and falls.

The sun climbs quickly, and gets warmer. Then the level of the river begins to rise too. The black, gliding water acquires yellow and white eddies, it licks more boldly at the lacework edging the banks—and when it finally pours over the shelf and down into the foundations of the palace, it does so in a cloud of spray with a gruff voice. Within the palace the first quiver of doom is felt.

The sunshine is stronger every day. The slope beside the ice becomes free of snow. The ice walls still stand in the sunshine, no longer part of the scene; abandoned by the snow they are helplessly out of keeping.

Slowly the palace changes colour. The shining green ice whitens in the warmth of the sun. The transparent chambers and domes grow dim as if filled with steam, veiling all they may possess, drawing a cover over themselves and concealing it. The whole palace draws the white colour over itself and starts to dissolve on the surface. Inside it is still ringing hard. The ice no longer sends out lightning among the fields, but shines, whiter than before, shines quietly. The huge ice palace is a single white mass in a brown and fallow spring landscape; it has drawn a covering over itself and shut itself in against its fall.

4

Melting Ice

Siss seemed to be standing on melting ice. There were grey floes and drift ice all round her. A black rent ran across the big lake one night—in the morning the water breathed long and deeply through it, and at once a small bird sat dipping its beak and drinking at the edge. Soon there were several more openings, and huge ice floes began to move without being able to advance; the outlet was not yet open.

Siss thought about the palace in the waterfall. What had happened on her last visit took on a different complexion after her conversation with Auntie; it must have been an hallucination. She had been so much on edge just then that she could have imagined a good deal.

The palace, too, was different since her shy conversation with the boy. It had in fact aroused a new desire to go there. Her conversation with the boy was recorded in her mind in lasting script. She would certainly not get to know him any better than she did now, and yet . . .

The boy had made the palace different—it was as it had been when the men stood there in the night. Once again it was for the sake of those men in the night.

The river is in spate, the boy had said. The palace is white. It will soon fall.

The ice palace stood quivering in a surging stream. It

would be crushed. It fascinated her. She felt she ought to go there.

Meanwhile she watched rent after rent appear in the thick, greying ice on the lake. The water lay grey in a naked, fallow landscape. No greening yet. In the mountains the mass of snow was great; an even greater spate of flood water was approaching. Then the palace would fall. There was something sadly fascinating in the thought: on a day with a fresh smell and a touch of mist—then it will shake the earth.

At school no approach was made. But it seemed to be in the air: soon there would be an opening. It had to come from Siss, but she still kept her distance. Then one day, since she did not summon up her courage, a note was lying on her desk: 'Aren't things going to be as they used to be soon, Siss?'

She would not look round to try to find out who had written it; instead she ducked farther down in her desk. Had they perhaps stolen a march on her?

Siss was under tacit observation. But she was approached openly too. The boy with the boot stood in front of her one morning, alone. Perhaps he had been sent, perhaps he was there on his own account.

' Siss—'

She was not unfriendly. 'Is anything the matter?' she asked.

' Yes. Things aren't the same as they used to be yet,' he replied, looking her straight in the eyes.

She felt a desire to touch him, or rather that he would do something of the sort. Neither made any move.

' No, it's not the same as it used to be,' said Siss, more

153

unwillingly than her expression warranted. 'And you surely know why. '

' It *can* be as it used to be,' he said obstinately.

' Are you so sure?'

' No, but it can be as it used to be just the same.'

She was glad he had said it, and yet . . . Her dimples appeared, but she stopped short and behaved as usual.

' Has anyone sent you?' she asked stupidly, without thinking. Did the rest of them tell you to say this? she should have said.

' No !' he replied, offended.

' No, of course not.'

' I can do things like this on my own.'

' Yes, I know that.'

But he was really angry, and would say no more, but turned abruptly away.

This was the small event that gave her the push. She had to do something at once now, take this step, overcome this feeling of shame she had towards them—even though it was curious that it should feel like shame. In any case she had cut herself off from them. It was a comfort to have Auntie's advice behind her now that it had to happen.

The palace in the waterfall gave her the chance to show them clearly how she felt. She would bring up the forbidden subject herself. The ice was ready to be crushed, the boy had said, and she wanted to see it before the river swept it away.

On the Saturday Siss made her appearance in the school-yard in a new way, and said to the expectant circle: ' Look, I have an idea. Shall we go to the ice palace tomorrow? It'll fall down soon, so I've heard.'

'Do *you* want to go?' said someone softly in amazement, but was nudged.

They were all amazed, and stood looking at each other. And then to the ice palace of all places, the very centre of this dangerous thing that they had been forbidden to mention? What has happened to Siss? was written all over them.

'What shall we do there?' asked someone.

Siss replied calmly and with assurance now that she had started. 'Only that it might be fun to see it once more before it topples down. It can topple any day now, said someone who had seen it. I believe it looks even more strange now,' she concluded.

The group had one or two leaders now. Two to be spokesmen in just such a situation. Siss was surprised to see that one of them was the boy with the boot, who had once seemed to pop up out of nowhere, and shown her goodwill. Now it appeared that he had become a leader. The other was the girl who had taken over after Siss. It was she who took the initiative.

'Are you making fun of us, Siss?' she asked. 'This is such a lot, all of a sudden.'

'Of course I'm not.'

'We hadn't expected you to say something like that, you see,' said the boy, to show his position.

'I know.'

'We can't be sure all at once if you're with us again, said the girl, 'but since you say so, then . . .'

They had Siss in the middle of them when they all went home. There was no noise. They walked along, keeping her in the middle. She did not dislike it either, she realized.

155

It was funny how excited you could be over such a quiet homecoming.

At home they asked casually what was going on? She told them about it at once; the flush of her homecoming made her frank. During the evening she noticed that she was sitting with Mother and Father on either side of her. Father began by saying, 'We've been waiting for the day when you would come home happy.'

Mother said : 'We knew the day would come. It wouldn't have been easy to live through this winter otherwise.'

Siss winced. But they said no more.

We know you've won through, they might have said, and made it embarrassing.

Of course she had made them unhappy this winter. But she knew it all too well, and needed no reminder. There was joy in the house now, but it was just as awkward to be in their company.

5

An Open Window

One is not freed by mere words. It was late on Saturday
evening—and it had diminished, the feeling that had
buoyed her up when she walked home with the group.

Siss lay in bed trying to prepare herself for the morning,
and was so excited about it that she could neither prepare
herself nor sleep. Tension, happiness and anxiety alter-
nated. She lay with wide-open eyes in the lamplight.

She was facing the window; a thin, white curtain was
drawn across it. All of a sudden she saw one of the casements swing open. Swing out into the darkness. What was
it? Nothing more happened. A slight movement of the
curtain in the draught, just as when you draw in your
stomach, then everything was still. No wind. But it must
have been the wind! The hook could not have been on—
but she seemed to remember having seen it so. And her
room was on the first floor of the house.

A window that opens by itself on to the night like that
—you think to yourself that it doesn't do it for fun or for
no reason at all.

Siss was immediately gripped by fear, and she was on
the point of calling through the wall. She stopped herself.
Let them enjoy their happiness in peace. They can do
nothing about this.

The night air streamed in through the aperture like a
cold cataract. She stared, paralysed, at the black opening

that could be seen through the curtain. What would come in? Nobody. It's not like that. Nobody comes in through openings like this, they only open.

She braced herself and said : This is nonsense, and you know it perfectly well. Of course it didn't open of its own accord, it's my imagination. There can't have been a hook on it, and it must have been a gust of wind I didn't notice.

But it is so unpleasant to see casements swinging open without reason. You don't know what is true and what is imagination.

Siss lay tense and calm at the same time. Not numb with shock, but prepared for more, should it come; letting it devastate her in the dark relapse she was in.

Her thoughts ran on. Tomorrow is my last day, flashed through her mind. That's why the window opened. There *is* something about that ice palace tomorrow. Something will happen at the palace. Fear can resemble a crackling sound in a frozen ditch. Her limbs felt curiously alien.

It was I who thought up this trip for them; I had no difficulty persuading them to come. But something will go wrong at the ice palace tomorrow.

It's the last day. The big white piece of ice is quivering. The river is pounding against it and will shatter it.

She could see it all. The whole group, excited, running about—although they did not share her secret experiences. They would climb all over it, out on to the roof, on to the domes of ice. She would call into the terrible roar that it was dangerous! but she would not be heard. They would climb out on to the roof and she herself would climb it first when it came to the point. They would signal to each other wildly out on the top that it was dangerous, and climb higher—but that would be the moment, as she had known; it was this the palace and the river had been waiting for, she had known it all along, now it would crash. They would stand out on top, she had drawn them all with her into this horror, gaping cracks would open beneath their feet, the palace would totter and fall forward under the pressure of the water with all of them on top of it, down into the seething channel, and that would be the end. She had known it all along, ever since the moment when the men stood there with their sombre song of sorrow.

As she fixed her eyes on the open window this took shape in her mind. She had no difficulty inventing it, it was there, she saw exactly what would happen the next day. Not in panic, but as a stranger watching—although involved herself.

Am I going to *do* this tomorrow?

Must I?

No, no!

There was a breathing from the quiet aperture. She did not go over and shut the window again. She was no longer afraid of the dark, but all the same she could not face reaching for the window with outstretched arm.

I'm not afraid of the dark, she had said to Auntie in parting, and at that moment she had not been afraid.

I must be afraid after all. I'm not going over to shut that window.

She had a couple of coats hanging in her cupboards. She fetched them and laid them on the bed so as not to get cold in the draught from the gaping aperture. She could not turn her back on it, nor switch off the lamp. She could not be in the darkness with the thought that it was open—she lay looking straight at it until she remembered nothing more.

6

Woodwind Players

The Sunday morning was frosty before the sun took hold in earnest. There was a slight crackle from frozen trickles of water on the dun-coloured fields when Siss left home. They had agreed to meet very early for their trip to the palace in the waterfall.

Siss did not turn and look back at her home—the numb wakeful night had not affected her to that extent. My last day? Nonsense. Now it was morning and one thought differently.

But for her it was a tense morning.

The water that had frozen was only the brittle silver ornamentation that forms among the grass roots on frosty April nights—the water did not seem to have paused, it left its trace on everything. It filled all existence, cascading in all the rivulets—its singing never so clear as on a holiday morning, whatever the reason. The big lake was brimful after the thaw, with a haze above it, large and small ice floes floating in it, and its shores black. Beyond it all, unheard at such a distance, flowed the great river, thundering with giant power.

A thunder that was familiar to Siss and that she was about to seek, with trepidation.

Anything but stop. The excitement of rising sap, the excitement of the scent of damp earth—her heart quivered as she walked amongst it all. Soft-toned, inciting woodwind players had come, enmeshing Siss in sad and joyful enchantment.

We are woodwind players, enchanted by things we cannot resist.

Everything is naked and new. A rock stands in running water. It sticks out, motionless, like a lifted axe, parting the moments for us, so that we can get there quickly enough. We are expected. A witless small bird plunges towards the rock and lies in the heather, then flutters up and does not appear again.

We are expected.

We are among the white stems of the birch trees before we realize it. One moment we were on our way, now we are here. We are expected. *The brief time left to us will be spent here.*

A bird passes overhead. A birch-clothed promontory runs out into the lake. Our brief time.

Siss said to herself : Today I shall go back to the others. Is that why?

What is why? The question seemed to come up against a blank wall.

It was not quite clear why.

Siss was out so early that she thought she would be first at the meeting place. It would make it simpler for her. She was going back to the others after shutting herself away from them—for that reason she wanted to meet them one by one as they arrived. To walk towards the whole crowd would take more courage than perhaps she had.

But as it turned out there was someone else who had

thought of being first, and was. When Siss arrived the reticent leader-girl was already there. Without a word and without anyone appearing to know why, she had taken control as soon as Siss had begun standing by herself at school. She was energetic and firm, and was immediately accepted. Siss had stood watching this through the winter, and had begun to long for her company, but had never approached her. Now she went forward composedly and nodded good morning.

Siss said : 'Are you here already?'

'I could say the same.'

'I thought it would be easier to be here when they arrived,' said Siss frankly.

'Yes, easier for you. I guessed that. That's why I left early. I wanted to meet you before the others got here.'

'What's it about?' Siss asked against her better judgement.

'Oh-h-h, about you know what.'

They looked at each other tentatively. They were not enemies, they both observed. Siss forced back her longing for companionship; that would have come later, if at all. She felt too that she did not have the upper hand. But the girl's face was unrecognizably tense; it had always been smooth and serene before.

'It was fun going home with you yesterday, Siss. I could see that everyone thought so.'

Siss said nothing.

'You too.'

'Yes,' said Siss softly.

'But you can't get out of it because of that,' said the girl, trying to steel herself.

'Get out of what?'

'Oh, I think you know. We must talk about this before the others come.'

Her voice was more strained. She persisted : 'It *hasn't* been fun this winter, Siss.'

Siss reddened.

The girl persisted : 'Why did you do it?'

' It wasn't *against* anyone. It wasn't like that—' faltered Siss.

She was about to say that she had promised, but remembered that the girl knew this well enough. Everyone must have heard about that promise. It wasn't any use now. The attractive girl said to Siss : 'We felt as if it *was* against us too. Surely you could have stayed with us?'

The leader-girl's eyes were scornful. Siss ducked and replied : 'I didn't think I could, so there. And so I didn't either.'

' And you stood there just the way she did.'

Siss flared up. 'You're not to talk about her! If you mention her, I'll—'

Now it was the leader-girl who was flushed and unhappy and who stammered, 'No, of course not! I didn't mean—'

But she pulled herself together quickly. She knew that the group whose leader she was had nothing to be ashamed of in this matter. Siss had made that test too and learnt a lesson from it. She drew herself up and looked calmly at Siss.

Siss felt the power radiating from her, sensed her strength. It had been hidden, but this winter it had sprung out into the daylight—it had happened in just the same way to the boy with the boot.

' You mustn't mind my saying this,' said the girl.

' No.'

'Are you sure?'

Siss nodded. *We* must get together, she thought.

The girl asked cautiously, 'What do you want to show us there?'

'At the ice?'

'Yes. There must be something.'

'There is, but I can't tell you about it,' answered Siss helplessly. 'You must come yourselves.'

'It all seems so strange when you talk about it.'

'None of you saw it, did you? You weren't there that night, were you?'

'No,' said the girl shyly.

They fell silent and stood there together. We shall stand here for a long time.

'I expect they'll be here soon,' said the girl.

'Yes.'

'What's the matter?'

Siss was nervous and altered. She looked at the seemingly strange girl standing there, the same age as herself. We shall look at each other in a mirror! she thought haphazardly. What's the matter? she had asked. A question at the very moment when she was off-balance, spellbound by her companion because the same thing was happening all over again. Siss said : 'Yes, you see—'

The girl waited.

Siss began again.

'You see, so much that's impossible is happening.'

'Yes, Siss.'

Nothing much. Just : Yes, Siss. Yet it went straight to the heart. We must get together somehow.

At once a wandering shadow came between them. She started and said headlong : 'But you mustn't come to me!'

'What?'

'And I mustn't go to you!'

'What?'

'*Or it will happen all over again,*' said Siss wildly.

The leader-girl gripped Siss tightly. 'Now don't go off again—we're with you. You mustn't go off again now.'

Siss only felt the blessed grip.

'Are you listening?'

'Yes,' said Siss.

The strong girl let her go. It could not last longer. Siss turned half away, tore at a willow twig and picked off the buds. There was a chattering just behind the trees and in spite of everything it felt like a liberation.

The stern girl said quickly : 'Here are some of the others. I'm glad—'

'So am I.'

They were surrounded by three or four others who arrived with happy faces.

'Hello, Siss.'

'Hello.'

Siss's plan, to meet them one by one, had come to nothing. The leader-girl made it impossible.

The rest of them arrived, and they started out.

The reticent girl said nothing now, merely mingled with the group. One of the boys was leading the way. Siss must have noticed him. Without being entirely aware of it, she skied beside him for a while. He had turned her over with his boot so kindly one miserable day. And since that day he had been a leader. He had been around on other occasions too, but they had not been like that day with the boot.

She found something to say.

' Is it you who knows the shortest way?'

' Yes,' he answered abruptly.

' Have you been this way often?'

' No,' he said in embarrassment, snubbing her.

Siss fell behind.

How ought I to behave today?

They radiated through the wood, scattering and coming together again. Siss noticed how they made her the centre of attention, and was ashamed. But it was not unpleasant. The stern girl seemed to have disappeared, using none of her authority. The others for the most part kept close to Siss, not saying much, for this was a solemn outing and they wanted to show they were aware of it.

No one let themselves go. If anyone started making a noise he was stopped by a hostile silence which he understood. They all knew that this was a memorial pilgrimage.

The ice palace stood for something special for Siss, they knew. Siss was going there and wanted them to come with her for some reason. They accepted this, and that was why it was no ordinary ski trip, but a solemn occasion.

Now they had reached the first valley.

They would be going straight across small valleys today. The sun had become strong and warmed the heather and last year's pale grasses. It smelt like some magic morning when one was quite small, and now it lay like ballast, heavy inside them. All that one did not yet know. There was a little of it in that smell. They moved solemnly, but the low tones of the woodwind players made their eyes wild.

Siss was kept in the centre. If she tried to move to one side they gathered round her again. She looked across at the bluff, silent leader-girl and thought: They mustn't.

In the first valley. Then up the slope—and there on the hill they knew you could see the waterfall in the distance. They hurried up the slope for that reason.

And there it was. Far away the great ice palace stood white in its frame of dark spring fields. It had not been crushed by the flood-water.

Siss felt their eyes on her.

' Shall we get our breath here?' she asked.

She did not need to, nor did any of this vigorous group, but they sat down for a while and looked over towards the palace and the waterfall.

Wasn't that right? The boy who had led the way was standing in front of her, asking her privately, ' Shall we turn back here?'

She shot up. ' Turn back?'

Had he seen correctly? Had she wanted to avoid something? What was she afraid of? She was not sure.

' Why do you ask that? Surely we're not going to turn back?'

' No,' he said, ' but in that case can't we go on?'

' Of course.'

There was no release yet for the group. They skied along in the same way as before, bound by the unusual event. In this fashion the little procession passed down into the second valley. The land sloped steeply downwards. The view disappeared at once.

But this time is for Siss.

They skied quietly and in silence. Anyone used to seeing them every day in the school-yard would not have believed they were the same people.

It must be soon now.

What will be soon?

Siss felt nervous down in the second valley. She knew what the outcome of this would be, that there was no way of avoiding it—and she wanted to be in this web in which she was entangled, she remembered.

She told herself nervously what was happening: I'm going back to the others.

In this valley, too, there was a brook to be jumped. They shot over it. They were in no mood for delays, and hurried up the slope once more—to the spot where they could see their goal again, and closer.

They had intended to go solemnly, but were in such a hurry that they half ran up the last part, as if compelled to get there in time before the ice palace collapsed. A nervous running.

Now they could hear the roar of the waterfall, not loudly below the crest of the hill, but as if it were rounding the crest and coming down to meet them.

Up on the hilltop they could see the whitening palace clearly, still some distance away, but enormous. It did not belong to this world, but still stood there for an unbearably long while, towering in front of Siss.

They were watchful towards Siss. The sight affected them all. The girl who was the leader came over to her and asked in a low voice, 'Do you want to turn back?'

They must all have been convinced that Siss was afraid of it. Here was the question for the second time.

'No, why?'

'Don't know—you looked a bit odd.'

'You're imagining it. Don't you all want to go there?'

'It's *your* trip, the whole thing, you know that.'

'Yes.' Siss had to admit that it was so.

'So we don't mind if you want to turn back here. You really did look as if you'd rather.'

'No, it wasn't that, I'm telling you.'

Siss looked helplessly at the firm, clear-headed leader who knew nothing about the memories she had of the ice palace.

'All right, as long as you want to.' The girl turned to the others and said they would go straight to the waterfall, and picnic there.

Down into the third valley. No one ran on ahead. Still the solemnity was not dispelled.

The ground was rough, with thickets and clumps of trees, down in the third valley. They could not help becoming separated as they picked their way forward. The usual brook, brimful of water, was here, with pools and small heads of froth.

Siss found herself alone behind a thicket—and at once someone came alongside. It was the boy who had led the way, now no longer at the head of the procession. She looked into his eyes, and saw that they were brighter than usual. She asked hastily, 'What do you want?'

'I don't quite know,' he said.

She felt his eyes on her all the time. He said: 'No one can see us here.'

Siss replied, 'No, no one in the whole world.'

'Let's jump across the brook,' he said.

He took her hand and they jumped across the brook together. It was strange, and then it was over. He held her little finger for a few paces after the jump. That was strange too; he noticed that the finger dug itself into his hand slightly. The finger did so of its own accord.

They let go quickly, and hurried round the thicket in order to join the others.

They were at the foot of the palace, and it was enormous : the pale white mass of ice, and the waterfall in spate. A cold, raw wind was blowing off the falls. The group went as close to it as they could. Their clothes rapidly turned the colour of grey silk from the spray. The spray rose up from the middle of the palace and rained down again. The air vibrated.

Their mouths opened in speech, but nobody could hear a word, only see mouths opening eagerly. It was too wet, and altogether too overpowering. They retreated to a point where they could talk.

A ring round Siss. They had brought her all the way there and they had done it successfully—they all stood wearing this expression. They were themselves impressed, by the enormous mass, and by the circumstances that had brought them there.

Siss was thinking compulsively about the men who had stood there. A dirge had been sung in the roar. It had grown and altered with the passage of time : now she remembered clearly that they had sung.

It was gone now. Was it in vain? No, no, it wasn't in vain; it will never be forgotten by those who stood here that night.

But the ice palace will soon be destroyed, and then it will look just as before, only the savage waterfall that concerns no one, that fills the air and shakes the earth and will never come to an end.

Everything will go on as before, Siss.

Somebody pulled at her arm—as she stood smarting with thoughts from which she could not free herself.

'Siss, don't you want to come and eat?'

'I'm coming.'

She awoke and saw a ring of friendly faces. They had all shown that they wanted her. And now they put aside solemnity.

In a while they were racing up the steep slope in the spray to climb to the top of the ice. On the slope they could see how the palace gripped the earth banks with huge claws of ice around the stones, into hollows and round trees. Even so, the waterfall would be strong enough to tear it loose. The wearing-down process was under way and must have reached its climax by now, but was invisible : a tug-of-war impossible to picture was taking place all the time.

Up on the top the ice was the same as anywhere else : white and pitted by the sun, not one transparent spot.

'Can we go out on it, do you think?' called someone above the din.

Siss started and remembered what she had reasoned out as she lay in bed.

'We mustn't, it's dangerous,' she said, but nobody heard her in the roar of the falls.

'Yes, of course we can!' shouted the boy who had led the way, and sprang out on it before Siss's very eyes.

They all stormed out. Siss was there too before she realized what she was doing. As soon as she set foot on it she felt the quivering in the huge block.

'Can't you feel it?' she shouted as loudly as she could. They heard nothing. They were all shouting just as loudly. All was noise.

'Hooray!' screamed someone, a shout so unfettered that they might have been standing on the severed ice palace, sailing with it downwards in the seething spume. 'Hooray.'

Their eyes shone strangely. They crawled about on the top, among the domes, in the grooves. They were a *little* cautious, not entirely blind to the danger, knowing they would never have been allowed to do this if any grown-ups had been with them. Siss no longer warned them; she was enjoying it herself, her eyes shining too. And then came the crack.

Bang! it exploded beneath them, in the foundations: an explosion or a blow or whatever it resembled. It might have been a hammer blow on a clock that needed one in order to strike. But it *was* a crack, a crack with destruction in the sound. In the impossible tension in which it stood, the ice palace had split apart somewhere. It was the first warning of death.

Loud above the din of the falls.

All of them out on the top turned white and made for dry ground on two legs or all fours, whichever was easiest. They had no desire to ride away with the ice when destruction overtook it; they wanted to live.

No, no! thought Siss too, as she saved herself. But it was as close as could be to what she had imagined during the night.

Once safe on the ground, they stopped to see whether its destruction would be completed. It was not. Nothing more happened. The ice stood. There had only been the one *bang!* from inside, and then silence. The river came pouring mass upon mass of new water from above, but the palace withstood the pressure.

Somewhat shaken they climbed down the banks of the

waterfall again, over-courageous too, since it had gone so well. Now they had something to talk about later. They were not ready to go. The ice palace still held them. Their eyes still glittered.

They glittered towards Siss too, but she could not meet them. The wild mood from on top had passed, couldn't they see that it was impossible to stay here? No, they couldn't, they had no reason to do so. For them it was an adventure.

Did they read her expression and were they disappointed with her? But they ought to have seen how impossible it was to stay here. The eternal roar of the waterfall filled the heavens and the earth, but still they could not fill one empty space. The others did not know this, they saw the adventure and their eyes glittered with it.

She stood up after a while and said, ' I can't stay here.'
Nobody asked her why.

The leader-girl came over and asked, ' Are you *going*?'
' No. Only a little way, just over there, to get away from it.'

' All right, we'll all come in a minute.'

Siss walked away slowly between the trees, where the way would lead back for them all.

No, I shan't go away from them now.
I've gone *to* them now.

She walked in among the trees and bushes and sat down on a stone. The wood was leafless and the slender trees were visible, stem upon stem, for a great distance. Siss sat beneath a steep slope, so that the roar of the falls was deadened, but the air still seemed to vibrate with it. Wild and unceasing. Unceasingly new, unceasingly moving on.

She thought of the consideration the others had shown her that day. When they catch up with me I must try to be different. How?

She sat on the stone and thought over the matter for a long time, waiting to hear the great crash behind her, telling her that now it was happening. It did not come; only the even roar churned on.

In any case it's over.

Everything is over here, it has to be.

Today I really shall break my promise.

It's because of Auntie that I'm doing it, that I can manage to do it. I still don't know whether I ought.

But I shall.

Thank you, Auntie.

I shall write to Auntie when I find out where she is.

She was not left sitting alone for long. The group did not come, but a dry twig cracked against the soft floor of the wood—and two fine lines passed through her : it was the girl and that boy. Both of them were coming.

The burden fell away. She got to her feet, her face a little flushed. There they were, both of them.

7

The Palace Falls

No one can witness the fall of the ice palace. It takes place at night, after all the children are in bed.

No one is involved deeply enough to be present. A blast of noiseless chaos may cause the air to vibrate in distant bedrooms, but no one wakes up to ask : What is it?

No one knows.

Now the palace, with all its secrets, goes into the waterfall. There is a violent struggle, and then it has gone.

A wild commotion in the empty, half-light, half-cold spring night. A crash out towards nothing, from the innermost holds that have worn loose. The dead ice palace takes on an echoing tone in its last hour, when it releases its hold and must go. There is a clangour in its struggle; it seems to be saying : It is dark within.

It is shattered by the pressure of the water and pitches forward into the white froth from the falls. The huge blocks of ice strike one another and dash themselves into smaller pieces, making it easier still for the water to seize them. It dams itself up, breaches the dam again, and tumbles downwards between the rocky banks of the broad channel, floating away and quickly disappearing round a bend. The whole palace has vanished from the face of the earth.

Up on land there are slashes and scars in the river banks,

upturned stones, uprooted trees, and supple twigs that have only been stripped of their bark.

The blocks of ice tumble away pell-mell towards the lower lake and are spread out across it before anyone has woken up or seen anything. There the shattered ice will float, its edges sticking up out of the surface of the water, float, and melt, and cease to be.